LIFE ON THE LION

MAGICAL MIDWAY PARANORMAL COZY SERIES, BOOK #2

LEANNE LEEDS

BADCHEN PUBLISHING

Life on the Lion
Published by Badchen Publishing
4500 Williams Dr., Suite 212-269
Georgetown, TX 78633 USA

LIFE ON THE LION

CHAPTER 1

"WATCH OUT!" GUNTHER YELLED AND WE BOTH dove underneath the table. After three months of magic lessons, I should be capable of levitating an object. Well, without turning that item into a fast boomerang.

The shattered mirror indicated this was not yet the situation.

"It moved," I told him as I wriggled out and stood up. "I mean, agree that I got it moving. That's improvement. Right?"

"Yes, you advanced so fast you nearly brained us, Charlotte."

"Technicality," I told Gunther. "It moved."

He sighed. The longer Gunther taught me, the

more he seemed to sigh. I wasn't doing *that* bad. Was I?

"It's all about *control*, Charlotte. I keep telling you that. You don't have to open the full magical fire hose for *every* single spell you do."

I always thought anything worth doing was worth doing full throttle. Considering the expression on Gunther's face, maybe I needed to rethink that.

Is it safe to come back in? Samson, my familiar, asked as he poked his head around the yurt flap. *I thought I heard glass breaking. Again.*

"Samson, let me clean up the broken glass off the floor. I don't want your paws to get cut up." I moved toward the broom leaning against the wall, but Gunther stopped me.

"I've got it," Gunther said. The heir to the rival Makepeace Circus pulled out his wand and waved it at the shards. With a yellow shimmer, the fragments disappeared. A moment later, the mirror reappeared in its frame. "You should remember things are a little easier to do sometimes with magic. Faster, too."

Show-off.

"Look, I get that this is more challenging than simply thinking something," Gunther said as he walked over to my love seat. "This will be harder for you to learn. The ringmaster power is nearly effortless to wield. This isn't. This is a skill you have to work at."

"I wouldn't call the ringmaster thing *effortless*." I plopped down in the chair next to Gunther with a crash. My mug of Mocha Elegance was lukewarm, but I took a big gulp, anyway. At some point, the elegance part of the drink had to kick in, right? "Yesterday, I had to redesign an entire yurt quarter. Three wereducks didn't want to share a bathroom. Try interior decorating when three ducks are quacking at you. Tell me how effortless it is."

"Look, I don't want to lecture you." Gunther held up his hands. "When I come next time, I want you to relax. Take it easy with the force you exert. It's like you're trying so hard you wind up squeezing the hose too tight. Instead of less power, you wind up with more. More than you can control at this point."

"I'll try," I told Gunther, and he smiled at me. "I appreciate you not lecturing me. I feel like a failure enough as it is sometimes."

"I mean well. Granted, I also don't want a skull fracture from a rocket-fueled hairbrush racing around your yurt." Gunther laughed. "I'm all about self-preservation."

"Speaking of self-preservation, how are you getting along with your Dad?"

And there it was. The walls slammed shut. Had Gunther gotten up and locked me in the armoire, it might have been more subtle.

Over the past three months, I mentioned getting an invitation to the Makepeace Circus multiple times. Gunther would clam up or change the subject every single time I said it. Eventually, I switched to inquiring about his father. His reaction was no better. At this point, I was considering just sneaking over there and looking around. I could get no insight into why Gunther was so defensive about his home. It was weird when he was so at ease in mine.

"Oh, it's all the same. You know, Dad is Dad. How's your Uncle Phil adjusting to the new situation?"

The new situation Gunther spoke of was that my Uncle Phil was dead. Upon his death, the Magical Midway ensconced me as the new ringmaster, and I held an ancient superpower that allowed this place to exist. At least I assumed it was old. It could have been born 200 years ago for all I knew. In any case, a super cosmic power hitched a ride on my person, and by doing so crowned me the undisputed leader of this traveling paranormal circus.

In theory, anyway.

I was *supposed* to be in charge. Like, magically chosen and anointed and infused with superpowers and all that stuff.

Though I was assumptively the leader, the old ringmaster, my Uncle Phil, still looked super alive for a dead guy. He knew the job inside and out. Everyone knew him for over twenty years. And now that he seemed utterly and entirely reanimated, for many here it was as if he had never died.

Heck, he looked better now than when he was alive. You don't gain weight when you're dead, no matter how many strawberry cream pies you eat.

Thanks to me, of course. Me, who would gain five pounds dipping my index finger in a dot of whipped cream and licking it.

But I digress.

I used my superpowers on my Uncle Phil's ghost. I thought it would be cool if folks could see and hear Uncle Phil. I mean, he was here anyway, and only I could see him. Why should I be the only one he bugged? I thought it would be a nice thing to do, make things a little easier. People missed him, and I hadn't been trained to be in charge of the circus, so win-win, right? I made his ghost visible and audible like the ghosts in the haunted house.

My uncle's girlfriend, Jeannie, then granted Uncle Phil's wish to have a body.

Poof! Instant resurrection.

Bam! Instant demotion for me in *everything* but incredible cosmic superpowers.

"What new situation? He's got everything he lost before his death. Well, except the ability to go off the fairgrounds."

"And the power, Charlotte. He doesn't have that anymore. *You* have that now. That has to be tough for him."

"Tough for *him*? You're kidding, right? The only thing that's tough for him is trying to find me so he can order me around like a super-powered windup toy."

"Charlotte!" Uncle Phil called as he burst into my yurt.

"See what I mean?" I told Gunther.

"Stand up, close your eyes, and ask to refill the hay bales, please," my uncle directed. He yanked me up out of the chair without waiting for my response. Glancing over at the love seat, he nodded to Gunther. "Good afternoon, young

Gunther. How's our girl doing with her magic lessons?"

"Just great, sir! Coming along fine." Gunther's eyes flashed to the mirror. Thanks, buddy. Gunther needed to learn to lie better.

"Did she break the mirror again?"

"You know, I'm standing right here! Do you want me to help or not?"

"Of course, Charlotte." Uncle Phil nodded. "It's not like I can pop out to the feed store, now, can I?"

I glared at my uncle. Closing my eyes, I asked for the hay bales to be refilled. Seconds later, I heard the small hiss of energy that told me the task was complete.

"Done. Anything else I can help you with?"

"Nope, everything's going splendidly, Charlotte. The big top show is completely sold out for tonight. The grounds are full of happy townspeople and profiting paranormals! All is as it should be, my girl."

"Awesome."

"I will see you later on today. So much to do, so many things to oversee! Ta-ta, my girl!" Uncle Phil sing-songed as he skipped out of my tent in his ringmaster outfit.

"Bye," I said to the already vacated space.

Gunther shifted in his chair and raised his eyebrow at me. I held my arms out and stopped just short of verbalizing the *I-told-you-so*.

"So, he's doing everything?"

"He knows everything, so he's doing everything. I'm a magical supply shop." I tried not to sound like a spoiled child with her toy taken away, but it wasn't working.

After his resurrection, Uncle Phil had tried to teach me how to run operations at the Magical Midway. I was too slow for his liking and…um… made the carousel disappear. Accidentally.

Then he *demonstrated* while I *watched*, insisting that an observational internship would be better for me. Eventually, he realized we could just *share* the responsibility. Because, really, where was he going? He took the aspects of the ringmaster that required expertise, and I got stuck with the elements that needed the power.

Hence my demotion to the Magical Midway supply closet.

"It might be a good thing for the moment," Gunther observed as he leaned in. "It gives you a chance to focus on other things. Like your magic."

"I guess." I shrugged. It was easy for Gunther to say. He had grown up at the Makepeace Circus and knew it inside and out. I didn't know what I didn't see. Three months after my elevation there were still people I didn't know well, yurts I never entered.

"I'm glad we get to spend time together, at least." Gunther smiled, and I smiled back. He had become a good friend, and a lot of fun to hang around. I was a little sad knowing that Gunther and I could never be more than friends. He was charming, handsome, and kind.

He was also completely off-limits.

I may only be the Magical Midway supply closet, but I still couldn't leave the fairgrounds for more than a day. Once Gunther became the Makepeace Circus ringmaster and anchor, he would have the same limitations.

Our time, like all good things must, would eventually end.

Fiona, Fortuna, Anya, Avalon and I got together for girls' dinner before the evening's circus show.

In the three months I had been at the Magical Midway, the five of us had assembled our own paranormal girl squad of a sort. A kelpie, a human seer, a naiad, a weredeer, and a ringmaster witch walked into a bar...

Then they drank and talked about guys.

A bunch.

"I can't understand why you and Gunther haven't...well, *you* know," Anya observed in her outspoken manner. She passed a sweet and savory concoction of fish she brought to the feast, and I snatched the platter. "He's sexy, you're cute. You spend so much time together, and it's not like anybody *here* will date you."

"Thanks, Anya, for pointing out my absolute lack of ability to appeal to a man. Any man. On this entire fairgrounds."

"That's *not* what she meant." Fortuna, the seer, reached forward to seize a roll. "No one may *treat* you as if you're the ringmaster since your Uncle Phil came back from the dead, but every man on these fairgrounds knows what you are. And that's setting aside the fact that most paranormals *wouldn't* date a witch, anyhow."

"That's witch bigotry." Fiona smacked her fist on the dinner table and hiccuped. Fiona had become fond of human wine.

"It is easy to be bigoted against the witches when they are bigoted against *us* by statute," the quiet weredeer alpha doe Avalon interjected and plucked at her salad.

"Hey, don't paint me with the same brush as the Witches Council. I assure you, I like you guys better than them. I'm not prejudiced."

"You're not," Fiona said. "You didn't grow up in their academies taking classes like 'Why Witches are In Charge of the Government 101.' We *lesser paranormals* are incapable of governance, don't you know." Fiona rolled her eyes.

"I'm not even supposed to be here," Fortuna pointed out. "Mark and I are both shut out of the paranormal towns by Witches Council regulations. They *hate* humans. At least they sure seem to."

I shook my head, disagreeing with Fortuna. "Okay, I have to stop you there. They don't do that to discriminate against you because you're human, they do that to protect all paranormals— witches, kelpies, everyone. Do you think if humans just tumbled into Mineral Springs they would smile, shake hands and go home again? They'd strip mine those diamond fields in a day. Maybe two."

"Ugh. She sounds like a member of the Witches Council. Spending too much time with the properly educated Gunther," Anya said. Fiona and Fortuna nodded and chuckled. Avalon looked concerned. Then again, Avalon always looked concerned.

"Look, I'm not suggesting the Witches Council isn't an unfair bureaucratic nightmare. I'm also not defending how they treat people. You guys well know I'm not a fan of the wicked triplets. Some of their laws, though, exist for a reason and it's for the preservation of all of us. Not *just* witches."

"Yes, but who determined that witches and witches alone would be in charge of the entire paranormal world? What makes them smarter, or wiser?" Fiona asked me. "I don't hold you responsible because witches took power and kept it for hundreds of years. I can tell you, however, it will be a sore spot with the rest of us."

"They were closer to humans," Anya told me. "They rose to power because they learned to pass as human before we did and because the humans believed them to be real at the time that the paranormal world reacted to safeguard itself. Witches were in the most danger, so it got them the most power and sympathy. That doesn't excuse what they did with it once they got it *one iota*." Everyone but me nodded.

I determined not to argue. I adored my girls crew of paranormal friends, but I knew my family was the only group of witches they had no problem with. The most disconcerting thing about becoming ringmaster had been the political conflicts within the paranormal world. I had never known about them, and their intensity surprised me.

My parents raised me in the human world outside the paranormal one. Their decision left me ignorant of the complications.

Until now, anyway.

Now, I had strolled right smack into them.

I was deemed a rogue witch by the ruling Witches Council for being born into a ringmaster family. Gunther was, too. My parents were frowned upon for living in the human world. And my uncle...

Well, my uncle was dead, so he didn't much care what anybody thought of him.

"This is a depressing conversation," I said and reached for my glass of wine. Like I said, I loved my friends and never thought twice about what type of paranormals they were. It made me uneasy when they mentioned their discomfort with witches, but it seemed like part of the price I had to pay.

Nothing more alcohol can't fix.

It tasted good even if I couldn't get tipsy anymore. Another fabulous benefit of being the ringmaster supply closet.

"True. Good thing we are insulated from that here." Fiona grabbed her wine glass and held it up in my direction. As she inclined her head, she hiccuped again. "For now, at least, we have an unbiased ringmaster, I think."

"Well, half a ringmaster. Maybe even a quarter," Anya grumbled. Ouch. That hurt.

"Jeez! Can't we go back to talking about cute boys?" I asked Anya. The skinheaded beauty rolled her eyes.

"You have to admit, Charlotte, your uncle is becoming more entrenched again as the leader of this circus," Fortuna told me. "You are doing little to tiptoe into his role anymore."

"I'm still trying to learn the magic Gunther is training me in, and I'm more worried about *that* than anything else," I told Fortuna. "I don't think I should advance beyond my capabilities. I'm too concerned about screwing up the way I did the first few days. Remember the story of the tortoise and the hare? I'm the tortoise. Step-by-step. No more shoving witches from the Council back to their homes in the blink of an eye. Or sending carousels to Egypt."

In my first full day as the ringmaster, three unpleasant witches came to visit. Asking no one, I sent them back to where they came from using my ringmaster power. Though my Uncle Phil had howled with glee at the action, I had broken the law by beaming them without their agreement. My father had to travel to Democritus and speak with a witch magistrate on my behalf, and he was scarcely successful in having the charges dismissed.

Ignorance of the law was a defense that could be used only three times, and I was determined to hold on to my other two passes. Just in case.

"Ugh. I hate watching powerful women abdicate themselves to a *man*," Anya snarled.

"That would be true whether that abdication was good for the woman, my friend," Avalon, the quiet weredeer told her closest friend. "You are a fierce defender of women. But part of respecting a woman's power, Anya, is trusting her decisions. If Charlotte does not feel she should step up fully yet, you must honor her choice."

"Yeah, yeah, yeah. So you keep telling me."

"You just want a woman in charge, and better if she deposes a man by force."

"Well, heck yeah, I do! You're damn straight."

"I *am* in charge, in a lot of ways," I pointed out to Anya. "I just think it's more important right now for me to learn about being a regular witch first. Once I've got that down, I can learn to juggle all the complexities of being the ringmaster operationally. Besides, I trust Uncle Phil and Samson. Don't you?"

"Anya loves your uncle, Charlotte," Avalon answered for the displeased Anya. "We all trust him. He did well by all of us for many, many years. My friend is just impatient for progress."

"Well, *I* am impatient for apple pie," I announced and got up from the table to retrieve the Costco apple pie my mother had sent from the oven. "À la mode, anyone?"

"The fact you have to ask, Charlotte, makes me question whether I *should* honor your leadership," Anya's voice cracked like a whip as all around the table laughed. "If you return to this table with no vanilla ice cream, I will lose *all* respect for your decision-making abilities."

"Can't have that," I said.

~

I stood in the shadows of the entry tunnel watching the show wrap up. The big top was full of beaming parents and howling children. Tiny, grinning faces were tacky with pink cotton candy. Some children curled up in their parents' arms trying to keep their eyes wide as sleep tugged at them through the loud chaos.

It made me feel wonderful, watching this. Proud.

I could sample audience members' energy like I was smelling single blossoms in a field. Happy, tired, merry, inspired, ecstatic...Most of the sentiments that swelled out from the humans that visited us were positive, more positive than you would feel from someone in everyday life. I was glad there were those left that still loved to watch such an old-fashioned show.

I contemplated how long this would endure.

If you were human, you saw the three rings filled with elephants and horses and bears and lions and tigers. All animals that, in the human world, were often exploited for entertainment. Two hundred years ago when my family founded the Magical Midway, few people cared for the suffering of animals.

In this modern day, humans had evolved. That was a good thing.

That growth, however, could spell the end of this place in the form it was. If humans would no longer visit, we would have no purpose. Our life as a traveling circus could end. The prospect disturbed me, but I had not figured out a solution for it.

"Charlotte," Bob shouted over the din of cheering and clapping. The Roman lares guard took my arm and leaned in so I could hear him. "Those three witches that came the first day you were the ringmaster. They are hanging out at the edge of the grounds. It looks kind of weird. They're just, like, standin' there. Doing nothing. Just staring."

"Thanks, Bob." I walked with him toward the back of the house where it was easier to speak. "How long have they been there?"

"I made that circuit twenty minutes ago, and they weren't there. So less than twenty minutes."

"Are they where the humans can see them?"

"Naw, they're at the back edge behind the big top. Behind the pretend generators." As a magically powered circus, we had a lot of things that weren't what they seemed. We worked hard to make sure the humans saw us as a run-of-the-mill circus. That included faking generators.

Okay, maybe not a run-of-the-mill circus.

Our acts and offerings were darn impressive. Way better than a human circus.

"Go back out there and keep an eye on them. I'll let my uncle know, and then I'll come out there with you."

"You got it, boss." Bob Larry grinned at me, saluted, and then raced toward the back exit.

When I first met Bob three months ago, I thought he was a little off. His brothers were the embodiment of controlled, serious Roman soldiers. Bob reminded me of a surfer dude from California, and I had little confidence in his skills because of his unusual personality. As I got to know him, I recognized he was whip-smart, and loyal.

He was also the only security guard that would speak in complete sentences. So, there was that.

I'm out at the back near the generator, Samson told me. *I can see them, and Bob was right. They are standing in a line and staring into the grounds.*

Why aren't they coming in?

Your ringmaster magic holds no sway over them outside the Magical Midway sphere. My guess is they're staying outside of the grounds so you can't send them back to where they came from. You still have two passes left with the magistrate, you know.

Wait a minute—I can't use my ringmaster magic outside the fairgrounds? I asked in shock.

At some point, I would know all the little rules surrounding what I could do and what I couldn't do. It didn't seem like that time would come soon, though.

You can, don't be preposterous, Samson scoffed. *You can use your ringmaster power anywhere. You simply can't influence anything not on the Magical Midway fairgrounds with it.*

That's one heck of a postscript, Samson. I took a deep breath and reminded myself again and again that I loved my familiar. I loved my familiar. I loved my ancient, intelligent, supportive, snide, secretive, headstrong, stubborn...

Okay, periodically I wanted to throttle him.

Like right now.

I would've thought it would be obvious. You are the Magical Midway ringmaster, not ringmaster of the entire world.

I zipped my mental voice.

As I strode out into the mild night air, I could see the three witches at the edge of the back clearing. I halted and crossed my arms, glaring. Sampling the energy of each woman, I read their impatience but little else. My power never showed me specifics unless people were projecting, and the three women guarded their objectives with efficiency. I cursed myself for not working on my talent more.

Uncle, we have company, I thought. I was thankful for the mental link that persisted between my uncle and me. Though it made me wonder why Uncle Phil went around the fairgrounds calling my name when he was looking for me.

Habit, dear girl. I'm heading out toward you, he called back.

I strolled toward the women, Samson beside me. Bob trailed behind me with his weapon at the ready. As I peered back, the intense look on his strained face startled me. Gone was his cheerful, dopey grin. Bob was all business.

"Welcome to the midway, ladies," I called as I arrived upon the edge of the defensive sphere. The shimmering wall of light between us, detectable only by paranormals, illustrated the divide. Mina, Mabel, and Mercy had visited me once before. When they couldn't manipulate the Magical Midway from me, they threatened to destroy it.

I was not happy to see them, but it didn't cost me anything to be congenial.

"You have *humans* here," Mina spat.

"We have hundreds of individuals here at the moment," I told the fiery redhead. "I'm not certain if you're aware, but we *are* a circus. There's a crowd of folks watching the end of the show as we speak."

"I am not speaking about the humans you allowed to pass over your border." Mina waved at the shimmering barrier. "I am talking about the two humans you have accepted as citizens. The humans you have living at a moderated paranormal property."

Mark Botsworth and Fortuna Delphi were two of the rare humans who contained an infinitesimal amount of paranormal blood in their heritage. When a descendant of a human and paranormal pairing walked onto the grounds of a paranormal circus, their inherent supernatural powers could awaken. Mark and Fortuna were two such humans.

"Fortuna and Mark? They came from the Langdon Circus," I told her, confused.

"And why do you think the Langdon Circus is no more?"

"Honestly? I have no idea. But I bet you're gonna tell me."

"The Langdons *defied* the statute. The circus was overthrown. The family elected not to pay the price for their sedition." Mina stepped forward, and the toe of her pointy shoe rippled the magic wall between us. Her eyes narrowed as she heaved herself up further with her own importance.

Bob Larry stepped closer and leaned his blade toward the women.

"I do not understand what you're talking about."

"Oh my gosh, she is *so* stupid," Mabel whined. "How does she not know there is a penalty for harboring humans in our world? It's like she knows nothing *at all*."

"What are you whining about?"

"Continue to conceal the humans and keep the boundary up, and you will pay the price for your disregard of the decree," Mina said. She held her arms wide as if to embrace the sphere that enveloped us. "Take this down, subject yourself to our orders, and your rogue family might be allowed to survive. Either way, the Astleys have restitution to pay that is long outstanding." Mina paused and crossed her arms. "Or perhaps you will allow your parents to pay the consequences?"

My heart froze in my rib cage. "Why them? They've done nothing to you!"

"Because we can get to them, stupid," Mabel answered. Mina slapped her and mumbled for her to shut up. "Um, because that's the law. They own the circus, too, stupid."

"I thought the law was no witch can harm another witch?"

"Well, we don't *kill them* kill them, you know," Mabel pointed out. "We could apprehend them. We could make them human, you know. Take all their witch power. You know, it's kind of like death. I mean, it's the death of a witch. They won't be *dead* dead. Just locked up. Or an icky human."

"They may as well be dead to you," Mina laughed. "Once imprisoned, they can't come here, and you can't go there. If they're human, well... you'd have to take a plane. Disgusting, filthy, dangerous things. You'd never see them, and you couldn't find them."

"Oh, for unicorn's sake, I know where my house is." Is she serious?

"What house? Doesn't your family circus trust pay for your filthy little animal shelter? Your home?" My jaw dropped at the sheer viciousness of this woman, and the glee she took in delivering her threats. She would've put many a Disney villain to shame. My confidence wavered.

I imagined the next statement out of her mouth would be plans for the coat she would make from the puppies we were housing.

"By *your own law,* we have seven days to answer!" Uncle Phil shouted as he ran up to us. "Charlotte, agree to nothing! Say nothing! Commit to nothing! For seven days they can do nothing."

"Is that right? Do they have seven days?" Mercy murmured behind Mina.

"I don't know, no one's ever argued before," Mabel told her.

Mina stared at Uncle Phil, and I could swear I watched her eyes turn red. The two stared each other down, one enraged and one confident. After several seconds, Mina shrieked and shot lightning at the sphere. It harmlessly bounced off —well, harmless for us. Mercy and Mabel dove for the ground squealing at their leader as the sparks rebounded.

"You should be worm food," Mina told my uncle once she collected herself.

"Magic is a marvelous thing, Mina. You

should try it."

"Insolent fool. I will return in seven days. I expect when I return you will hand over the humans and take down the protection around the Magical Midway that blocks you from us," Mina pronounced. "Until then, no harm will come to your parents. We follow the laws since we are the law."

"Just so I have all the facts here...If we gave you Mark and Fortuna, what would happen to them?"

"Why, *they* would be *killed*, of course," Mina said pleasantly. "No human can know of our existence and live."

Mercy's head snapped toward Mina. She stared at the woman as if Mina's statement had startled her, her face troubled. In the blink of an eye, Mercy's expression returned to a sneer. She shifted her eyes toward me, and I wondered if I had seen the concern at all.

"And that's, like, *dead* dead. Like, really dead. In case you're wondering," Mercy said as she tossed her blond hair. Mabel nodded.

"Seven days!" Mina shouted. The three women raised their arms. Lightning bolts flew from their fingertips, and fog surrounded them.

Then they disappeared.

CHAPTER 2

"Everybody, I need you to calm down! Be quiet!" I hollered at the assembled paranormals jostling against one another around my dining table. Fortuna and Mark sat against the wall looking glum with their heads down. Despite the crisis being provoked by their presence, they seemed to be the only two people without an opinion.

Word had spread through the Magical Midway of the Witches Council visit and threat. After my uncle and I reassured as many as we could, we called for a meeting the following morning. Besides Mark and Fortuna, my girl squad was in attendance. Bob stood back observing the crowd, ensuring no one got too out of control. Serena, a werelioness, perched next to Mark Botsworth, holding his hand. Her gray eyes revealed her fear even as her posture was rigid and defiant.

"How did they find out that humans were here?" Serena demanded. Her majestic voice cut across the chaotic din of chattering noise, and the room fell silent.

"The Witches Council has always known that humans are in residence at the circuses. They noticed the awakening power in the second-generation of the fairs," Uncle Phil told her. "It appears they are moving against us with much more seriousness than I expected. That's the only reason I can see for this. There's no reason I can think of to make it an issue all of a sudden."

"I do not wish to start a war with the Witches Council," Serena told him. "However, I will happily tear out the throat of anyone who seeks to harm Mark." The polished beauty leaned over to caress Mark's shoulder with her cheek. Mark raised his head and smiled at her, then pressed his head against her golden hair.

"Serena, I don't want to cause anyone harm, or for anyone to be harmed because of me," he told her.

"That is not up to you," she responded sharply.

A low, throaty growl emanated from her, even as her rich voice spoke the next words. "I am a lioness. I fight for whatever male I choose. And I have chosen you, human. With that, it is done." Mark's eyes filled with tears, and I heard his breath hitch as he bowed.

"We have seven days, so before we talk about tearing out people's throats, I think we should explore less violent options," I pointed out.

"I don't know, I think the violent solution deals with the issue," Anya chimed in and placed a hand on Serena's shoulder. "They're not men, but I bet I could drown the other two. Might be interesting just to *hold* someone under the water instead of chanting to them. I mean, that could work. Might even be fun."

I stared at my friend and swallowed. Sometimes I was thrilled Anya liked me, if for no other reason than it seemed far safer to be on her good side. This was one of those moments.

"We have a spy problem," Fiona said. "Whether it's the Makepeace spies, or the Witches Council spies, none of this would be happening if someone wasn't providing our enemies information. That has to end. We have been tolerant of the spy network, but times have changed. The spy network is no longer the charming gossip tree of a bygone time."

"I agree," Ningul said as he sat beside her. Of *course*, the centaur agreed. Ningul was so smitten with Fiona that if she reported to him the sky was made of blue cheese, he would've agreed with her. "It would seem that exposing and driving out the spies at the Magical Midway must take place."

"If they come back in seven days, centaur, and wipe out this place, spies won't matter," Costin, an elf from the bow and arrow show, pointed out. "That may be what led to this trouble, but the removal of them now solves nothing."

Aldo Forrest, a werebear, and Rhodia Adolphus, a werewolf, continued to sit at the side of the table without comment. Patches Timbo, the leader of the were-elephants, also said nothing. The weres kept to their own kind, so I knew none well. Other than Serena, with a personal stake in the outcome because of her relationship with Mark, the weres in the room quietly listened.

"I have *eight* children I need to protect," pointed out Krog Kobold, the goblin that ran the children's petting zoo. He slammed his hand on the table. "If we will have to run, I need to know now."

"We *all* have family we need to protect, Krog," Patches Timbo told him quietly. "So long as the barrier is up, we are protected."

"Are we *sure* about that?" Krog asked.

"Perhaps we should allow the ringmaster to speak," Ari Riddle said. "This situation may not be all that bleak. Ringmaster, can you perhaps explain whether we are all simply panicked in vain?"

The entire table of nearly twenty paranormals turned to stare at my uncle.

Except for Anya.

Good old Anya.

It is not meant as disrespect, Charlotte, Uncle Phil thought as he looked across the table into my eyes. I nodded.

I don't know the answer, Uncle Phil. So, at the moment they are all looking at the right person. My ego is the least of my problems right now.

While that wasn't entirely true, we needed to get on with a plan. My bruised ego could wait until later.

"From where I sit, there are two issues. One is the safety of Fortuna and Mark. If the witches cross the barrier, they have their magic. They can do damage. They can grab them. If they cross the barrier, it is quite true that Charlotte can do more to them than they can do to her. That is, no doubt, what made them reluctant to cross last night," Uncle Phil said. "But we would have to *catch* them here and hold them until Charlotte arrived."

"We will step up patrols," Bob Larry said.

"That's good, but you guys can't be everywhere, Bob," I told him.

"Charlotte, can you just do some protection spell on Fortuna and Mark?" Fiona asked.

"I can, but I don't know if we should count on that." I stood up. "In the human world, there's a saying that the good guys have to be right every time. The bad guys only have to be right once. I would have to come up with protection that covered every possible means of attack against Fortuna and Mark. I would only have to miss one thing, miss one possibility they thought of. I think it's safer not to rely on magic here."

"Especially not *her* magic," Clancy, the surliest of the leprechauns, grumbled under his breath as he jabbed his thumb at me. Anya turned and glared at him. He stuck his tongue out at her and rolled his eyes. "What? Everybody's thinking it. She's no Phil Astley. And *he's* not even Phil Astley anymore."

"Mark will stay with us," Serena announced.

"My sister will have no problem with it. We have no need to rely on magic to defend ourselves, and no witch can cast faster than my claws can tear the muscles from their bones."

No one disagreed with her.

"Fortuna can bunk with me," I said. "We can move the fairgrounds to a more defensible location, and we'll close to humans for the next seven days. I don't want to have to worry about protecting Mark and Fortuna *and* making sure the visiting humans are okay."

Uncle Phil nodded. "I think that's a good idea."

"What about the second problem?" Aldo Forrest asked. "Not that I don't care about the safety of the two humans, but my *immediate* concern is my clan. We are only four bears strong now. I aim to increase that number, not shrink it from a witch war."

"The second problem has two parts," Uncle Phil told him. "The immediate threat to the Magical Midway, and the longer-term threat. Even if we resolve the current attack from the Witches Council, it is clear that it won't be their last attempt. Charlotte, Samson, and I need to consider this carefully."

"You are not alone," Avalon whispered. She rose regally from her chair. "While you are our rulers, and we are obligated to your family, recognize you are a part of each of our clans. You have always dealt with us fairly, as have your forefathers. We honor you. You are not alone."

The shy leader bowed her head, and all those assembled followed. My eyes teared up as I gazed over the room. I glanced to the other side and caught Uncle Phil's gaze. I could see he was as moved as I was.

When they straightened, we bowed to them in response.

"Thank you, my friends. It is good to know Charlotte and I are not alone."

"We are totally, completely alone in this," Uncle Phil said once everyone had left the area. I gawked at my uncle in confusion.

"What do you mean we're alone? What was that big, spontaneous, sentimental bowing circle just a minute ago?"

"Comfort. Not truth."

He walked across the room and poured himself a drink from a flask he carried in his right breast pocket. Apparently, being dead did not stop Uncle Phil's imitation body from getting tipsy. Lucky him. I could use a drink right about now, too. Not that it would make a dent in my anxiety considering the ringmaster protections.

He is right. The Magical Midway is not untouchable. There is a reason that the paranormals hide within here, but are not entrusted to defend it, Samson said.

"I thought it was invulnerable? I thought that was the *whole* point?"

As you said, the good guys must be right all the time. The bad guys only must be right once. The circuses have been protected for several hundred years, but I can recall no time when the Witches Council has made such a concerted attack.

"Something has shifted," Uncle Phil said. "The Council has never made such an open declaration of war."

"Is it because of me?"

"I don't see how it could be because of you, my dear," Uncle Phil said. "You're not exactly an intimidating witch even with the power. No offense."

"Offense taken! Jeez."

What your uncle is trying to say so clumsily is that the Witches Council only attacks when they see something they want, or when they perceive a hazard. Your skills are not so honed that you represent a particular threat, so we have no reason to believe they are attacking for that. While they have always wanted the ringmaster power, we are unaware of any reason for the sudden desperation.

"Is it just us? Are they going after the Makepeace Circus, too?"

"I don't know. Have you asked your spies?"

"What spies?"

"The spies we have at the Makepeace Circus," Uncle Phil said matter-of-factly.

"I remember you saying that we have spies there. Or someone did. Maybe Gunther told me? I don't know, anyway, I know nothing about it. Like who they are, how to contact them. You know, stuff like that?" I raised my eyebrow.

"We have a centaur and a goblin. You can call them with the cauldron. Well, *you* wouldn't call them with the cauldron. You must get Ningul or Krog to call them. If you appeared calling one of them, it would be clear to their compatriots they were spies."

"That makes sense. Let's do that first. Do we need to warn Mom and Dad?"

"The witches can do nothing at all against us for seven days. For now, I think your parents are safe. Let's not worry them."

I grabbed Ningul (and Fiona, because Ningul and Fiona were joined at the hip these days) and headed to the communications yurt. Uncle Phil and Samson were waiting for us.

"So, what do we want to know?" Ningul asked.

"Just ask him if the Witches Council is making any moves or threats against the Makepeace Circus," I told him. "If the answer is yes, obviously, I want to know as much as I can about the situation over there."

"Her."

"I'm sorry?"

"The centaur spy we have at the Makepeace Circus is a female. Reina Ajax."

"Oh. Right, sorry."

"Be glad that Anya wasn't in here," Fiona pointed out.

I snickered. "I'm all for female empowerment, but man, she takes it to a whole new level."

"Let's focus, ladies," Uncle Phil said. "We're on an ever-ticking clock here."

"You're right. Go ahead, call Reina."

Ningul spoke to the cauldron, and I heard its familiar bubble. The room filled with the heady scent of irises as the steam rose.

"I am unsurprised at the timing of this call, Ningul," a pretty brunette woman said from within the steam. "I am alone, so you may speak freely."

"Why? Is something going on over there?"

"Aye, the paranormals of this place are more frightened than they usually are." Fiona and I glanced at each other with concern. Why would the paranormals at the Makepeace Circus *normally* be frightened? What was Gunther hiding?

"What's going on?"

"Three witches arrived last night at the edge of our fairgrounds. Though Roland Makepeace ordered all the residents to stay away from the area, a few overheard the conversation. The rumor is that the Witches Council has made it a priority to ensure the end of the Magical Midway. They have raised the penalty for harboring humans in paranormal towns and applied that to our nomadic lands as well."

"Are they coming after the Makepeace Circus as well?" Ningul asked unprompted.

"There is a concern here that Roland Makepeace has brokered some deal with the Witches Council to protect the Makepeace Circus while condemning you. While that deal protects the Makepeace inhabitants from this law, they fear it will cause outright war with the Magical Midway and imperil them all the same. The penalty for breaking this new law as a supernatural is...suspiciously severe."

"What used to be the penalty?" Ningul asked Uncle Phil.

"While humans have *been* forbidden, it was previously a fine. It's never been *that* serious a violation because we were the only ones doing it. The Council also looked the other way because of the likely paranormal heritage of the humans we allow to stay. Since pure humans cannot enter paranormal towns, anyway, this hasn't been a big deal."

"It looks like it's a big deal now," I told my uncle. "Can you ask Reina what the formal penalty is for paranormals caught? They didn't mention that to us."

Ningul posed the question to Reina.

"Imprisonment. Imprisonment for those that harbored the human, those who knew about the human harbored and did not turn them in, and confiscation of the property the human was harbored within," Reina told Ningul.

"This was *just* passed? It's a new law?"

Ningul relayed my question, and Reina

confirmed that the Witches Council told Roland Makepeace the law was new. Passed unanimously, and signed three days ago.

"If this *only* applies to us in practicality, this is a *direct* attack on us. They don't just want the Magical Midway, they want to throw everyone here in jail. That's ridiculous."

"I think that's a safe assumption to make, dear girl. Perhaps now that there are only two circuses left, the Witches Council feels safe enough to come after us," Uncle Phil said. He strolled over to the sitting area and sat down. The skin on his chubby face was tense, his brows knitted together in deep thought. "And we are really only one. Roland Makepeace would never join with us, and it sounds quite likely that he may be working against us."

"Aye, but do we *really* think that?" Fiona asked quietly. "Roland Makepeace is a right doaty, but we are the last two of our kind. Would that man really help those women take us down? Truly?"

The bubbling of the cauldron echoed gently in the silence as we all looked at one another. Each of us was looking for just one face filled with disbelief instead of nervous apprehension.

A wolf howled somewhere outside the yurt.

CHAPTER 3

FIONA, NINGUL AND I SAT IN THE communications tent until late into the night. After midnight, Fortuna and Mark poked their heads in and asked if they could speak. Waving them in, I glanced at Fiona. She snuggled deeper against Ningul's side and tucked her feet up beneath her.

"We both wanted to come see you and offer to leave," Fortuna said. Mark nodded as he squatted down on the floor near the coffee table.

"Neither one of us want to be the cause of the circus coming under attack. But we do both have lives that we can go back to, though those lives were not as full and genuine as the ones we have here."

"Whether or not you are here tomorrow morning, it sounds like it won't make a bit of difference to the wicked triplets," I told them both. "We have already broken their newly created law. My question would be whether you two *want* to stay here. Your lives are being threatened here. What do *you* want to do?" I asked them.

"I can't leave Serena," Mark said softly. "Yet I also don't know how I can stay and put her through all of this. If I have to, I can go back to my life as a teacher. This would certainly give me a new perspective on mythology in the lecture hall."

"I can do what I do now," Fortuna said. "It would just be a bit lonely. I would miss you all. Surely, though, they wouldn't come after us if we left."

"I don't know that you are correct about that," Fiona told her friend. "You know of us. That's not allowed. If you left, I think they would come after you."

"I also don't think it would keep them from coming after us," I added.

"We don't want anyone to get hurt because of us," Mark said.

"I think you underestimate what our kind has

had to deal with over the generations, Mark," Ningul said quietly. Fiona frowned and nodded as her boyfriend reassured the mentalist. "We are trapped between the human world and the witch world, and again between the witch world and the circus world. We have become used to being on the outside, have grown used to being threatened. If you speak to Serena, I suspect you would find that she will happily take up this fight with you."

"We are a tribe, ya kin?" Fiona told him and then yawned. "You are part of this tribe, too, wherever you came from. Even if you haven't been here that long. Even if you're human."

"Forgive me for saying so, but in that meeting of the leaders it didn't sound like we were all that welcome anymore."

"People are alarmed," I told Mark. "Heck, I'm a little uneasy. There has to be a way to solve this without going into an all-out war with those women, though."

"Maybe I can help." Gunther Makepeace stuck his head into the communications yurt and waited for me to wave him in.

"What on earth are you doing here at this hour?"

"I made a copy of the law they're trying to get

you guys on," Gunther said. He reached into his pocket and pulled out a yellowing piece of parchment with grand ink flourishes. "I heard they refused to come on your grounds, so I figured you might not have seen the actual law. Maybe it would help."

As I took the paper, Fiona leaped to her feet and ripped it out of Gunther's hand before I could touch it. "Your father give you this to give to our ringmaster?" Fiona shouted, waving the paper in front of his face. "Poison on the paper, maybe? Is the paper cursed so your father can hear all of our discussions?" Gunther winced as Fiona poked his rib cage. "Come on, *Prince* Makepeace, tell us why you are *actually* here in the middle of the night."

"Fiona, come on." I reached for the paper, and she yanked it further away.

"No, *you* come on," Fiona said and pointed at Gunther. "That's the son of the man that met with those wicked women not a full day ago. What do you think they were gabbing about, the latest circuit profits? Their new were-elephant?" Ningul reached out for Fiona, but she shook him off her and ignored his attempts to calm her.

"I would never do anything to hurt Charlotte,

Fiona. Come on, you know that." Gunther's face reddened at her allegation.

"You are a *Makepeace.*" Fiona shook her head. "I don't trust you at all, Gunther. Not with this. You are your father's son. If it came down to choosing between Charlotte and Roland, none of us doubt whom you would choose."

Gunther stood frozen to his spot only three steps into the room. His face flexed and twisted as if he wanted to talk to us but couldn't quite figure out how to say what he had to say. Finally, he sighed. "Perhaps coming here tonight was a mistake."

"Perhaps coming here *at all* was a mistake. Perhaps it was *you* that gave your father the idea to attack us like this," Fiona snapped. Ningul grabbed his fiery girlfriend and pulled her back, whispering in her ear something I could not hear.

"My father had nothing to do with the Witches Council law change," Gunther said as he rubbed his temples. "In fact, it *was* my father that suggested I come over here and bring you the law parchment. I know my father is not the kindest man in the world, and he won't win any popularity contests, but he wouldn't do what you're accusing him of!"

Fiona dropped the parchment to the ground

and frantically wiped her hand on her pants. Glaring at Gunther, she grumbled under her breath about poisoned papers.

"Okay, then why would he help us?" I asked Gunther. "Your father can't stand us."

"True," he agreed. "Once they are done coming after you, though, they'll come after us next. Dad feels the best defense for Makepeace is to ensure that the Magical Midway is not brought down by this."

"Daddy offering any *help* beyond the paper?" Fiona asked him. Gunther paused, then nodded no. "Thought so. This could be a dupe, Charlotte."

It *could* be a trick, though if it was a trick, the trick was not Gunther's.

Gunther always struck me as kind, honest, and I wasn't getting anything from him that indicated he was any different than usual. My concern wasn't that Gunther was lying, though.

My worry was that Gunther was being played by his jerk of a father. Even if Roland sent Gunther over here to trick us, he was likely unaware of his Dad's ulterior motives. Gunther would believe in his father's sincerity long after there was a reason to suspect he was a liar.

Fortuna and Mark watched me as I looked at my friend and magic teacher. Ningul held Fiona both for comfort and to prevent her from stepping up on Gunther again.

"How about you and I take a walk?" Gunther nodded.

"Charlotte, you can't—"

"I'm completely safe at the Magical Midway, Fiona. I won't eat anything, touch anything, or lick anything, okay?" Fiona smirked despite her mistrust, and Gunther blushed.

The Magical Midway was quiet. Despite the drama and uncertainty the residents had over the threats from the Witches Council, a tranquil calm had descended. Most people had withdrawn to their pavilions and yurt villages. Gunther and I strolled through the backyard toward a gazebo I had installed at the corner of the living area.

"Is this going to turn into some magical cage?" Gunther joked, stepping into the gazebo. "Some truth spell for those inside? Sound transmission to all the inhabitants?"

"It's just a gazebo, Gunther," I told him as I followed. "No tricks, no magical traps. Just a nice place to sit and chat."

We sat in silence for a while listening to the

breeze rustle the canvas. Far off drunken shouts of revelry periodically pierced the calm. Finally, Gunther spoke as he went on gazing into the distance. "I really thought with my coming around the past few months your buddies would have thought better of me by now."

"Two hundred years of struggle and mistrust is not a simple thing to get over in a few months, Gunther. And your Dad was kind of an idiot." I gazed back toward the yurts. "They're afraid. Things have changed here since I became ringmaster. They have two ringmasters, and now the Witches Council is jeopardizing their home. Something they all know your father did just a few days after my uncle died."

"My father offered to buy your circus, Charlotte, not scorch it to the ground."

I didn't know how to respond to that. I recalled the exchange with Roland Makepeace a little differently than his son did. Technically, Gunther was right, but the stream of taunts that fell from Roland's mouth against the Magical Midway made me wonder why he wanted to buy it if he detested it so much.

"Okay, let's change the discussion a little bit. What do you know about the conversation that took place between Mina and Roland? Did you overhear anything? Did your Dad talk to you after the Witches Council left?"

"I didn't hear much," Gunther said. He stood up and leaned against the large gazebo railing. "They showed up at the edge of the clearing behind our big top. The three of them walked in and told the gargoyles that they demanded to see the ringmaster."

"Gargoyles?"

"You have lares as security, we have gargoyles. Anyway, the gargoyles showed the three witches to my father's cabin. I stood out front on the porch to ensure that no one came in while they were meeting, but Dad lives in an old-fashioned log cabin. The walls are really thick, and I couldn't hear anything that was going on."

"Any thumping, banging, yelling you couldn't make out? Any shimmering through the window to indicate that magic was being cast?"

"No, nothing like that."

"How long did they all talk?"

"About fifteen minutes."

"That's a pretty long discussion when you think about it, Gunther."

A tiny mew broke into the exchange from Gunther's pocket, and his kitten's little head popped up. Delilah mewed again and tapped her tiny paw against Gunther's lips. "Is your kitten okay?"

"Yeah…" Gunther said as he peered at the tiny black cat. "She…um, she was in the cabin. When my father talked to the Witches Council." Delilah crawled out of his pocket and hopped onto his shoulder, chattering excitedly. "He seemed okay. He and Mercy hugged."

"Why would she hug him? Do they know each other well?"

Gunther stared off into the distance for a great while as his kitten kept chattering at him, but he stopped relaying anything she said. He scratched her head and nodded repeatedly. The little kitten seemed upset.

"Gunther?"

"I don't know."

Gunther was lying to me.

Samson, can you hear me?

Yes.

Can you come out to the gazebo? I need you to tell me what Delilah is telling Gunther. His kitten was in the cabin with the Witches Council and Roland. She's chattering like crazy, but he's not saying much.

On my way.

Where are you, by the way?

Checking for suicidal mice in the hay storage area.

Ew, Samson, gross. How do you know the mice are suicidal?

They are suicidal if they let me see them.

Stop chasing mice and get out to the gazebo.

I said I was on my way. You need not repeat your requests twice. I'm not a dog.

I watched as Gunther and Delilah engaged in an exchange I was completely locked out of. The tiny cat hopped from his shoulder to his head, nuzzling his ear as she chattered and meowed. Periodically, Gunther nodded and scratched her behind the ears, but he didn't explain what he was discovering.

Here we are. Samson hopped up on the gazebo wall. *What's the chatterbox blathering on about?*

I was hoping you would tell me.

"Hello there, Samson." Gunther nodded at my familiar. Delilah purred and rushed down from Gunther's shoulder. The little cat raced along the gazebo fence to rub against Samson in greeting. Samson touched his nose to hers and sat back on his legs while she accosted him. "Delilah's happy to see her buddy."

"I meant to ask you. Your father has a familiar, too? An official circus one like Samson?"

"No," Gunther shook his head. "The Makepeaces don't have a guardian the way you all have one. We just have regular familiars like any other witch."

"I never had a familiar," I pointed out. "My parents don't have one, either."

"They live in the human world. Witches that live in the human world aren't allowed familiars."

"What did you call Samson? A guardian?" Gunther nodded. "What's a guardian?"

"A long-lived paranormal animal that survives through generations. Usually, guardians are powerful supernatural beings, like a dragon or unicorn. Not sure why you guys only got a cat."

Can I bite him?

Come on, Samson, admit it. A dragon would have been cool, I teased.

Now I'm going to bite you. You're lucky any guardian would step up and take on the responsibility for this insane family. Animal shelters, circuses, witches living in the human world, the Witches Council attacks. You're not precisely a low-maintenance family, you Astleys.

Is there some job board for guardians?

Hush, the young one is saying something.

"I know! Stop worrying, Dad will figure something out" Gunther exclaimed, shocked, as he stared at his familiar. The little cat mewed in response and seemed to shrug.

What happened?

Delilah heard Mercy apologize to Roland Makepeace, that despite her oath to protect him, there was no longer anything she could do. Said if Roland had been a cat, all his fur would have jumped straight out.

Mercy? The dimwitted one?

The one that rarely speaks. Yep.

"What did Mercy oath to your father that she had to break?" I asked Gunther. His eyes shot over to me in surprise, and then he looked at Samson. With a frown, he shook his head no.

"I don't know."

There's a lot that boy doesn't know, Samson thought.

Or that he doesn't want to say.

"I have to go," Gunther said as he scooped up his tiny kitten and dropped it back into his pocket. "Look, I got you the law. I hope you can use it, and I promise, it's not poisoned. I need to go talk to my father. I'll be back by in two days for our lesson." Gunther squeezed my wrist, smiled, and turned to hop down the stairs.

"You still want to have a magic lesson this week? With all this stuff going on?" I called after him as he hurried away. "Maybe we should skip it this week."

Gunther stopped running and stood still, facing away from me. The stillness of the cold night air held me suspended, staring after him. After what seemed like an eternity, he turned and walked back.

"You can't put this off," Gunther said as he stepped closer. "Things are happening incredibly fast all of a sudden, Charlotte. Incredibly fast. I don't want to see you get hurt."

I stared up at his face. Gunther was so close that the aura of him invaded my space, and I felt a little drunk from it. We stared at one another quietly, and I regarded for the first time how extraordinary his eyes were. How long his eyelashes were. The air blew my hair across my face, and he reached up to gently wrap it behind my ear. Shivering at his gentle touch, I stepped backward.

"Promise me you'll practice, and you'll make time in two days when I return," Gunther demanded, his voice low. "I mean it, Charlotte. I worry about you."

"What do you mean everything is happening fast? What's everything?"

"I'll see you in two days," he bowed, spun, and sprinted into the night. I tried to ignore the flex of his powerful shoulders as he grew smaller and smaller. With a flash of light, he was gone.

He is a nice looking young man, Samson mused.

Shut up, cat.

~

"Did you find out anything?" Fiona asked when I stepped back into the yurt.

"Yeah," I told her and sat down. "That I get attracted to the wrong guys at the most awkward moments."

"I could have told you that you were attracted to him months ago." Fortuna passed me a cup of tea. "I didn't even need my gift to see that happening."

"He looks at her like she's—" I threw a stuffed animal at Fiona's head to cut her off, but it failed to lodge in her running mouth, and she kept going. "What? How you *can't* see that the two of you will wind up together is completely beyond me. Well, you would if he wasn't the son of Roland Makepeace, in any event."

"Stop it. We're friends. He just looked good in the moonlight," I said, taking a sip of the warm tea. "Like, fantastic."

"Well, while you were off cuddling with the

enemy in the gazebo, we've been looking over this law," Fiona told me. She waved me over to the table. The group had rolled out the parchment and weighted it with books, and were staring at it as if trying to interpret code.

"It seems pretty clear. Any privately held property harboring residential humans is subject to forfeiture. Any paranormals aiding the harboring of the humans are subject to punishment up to and including imprisonment or death."

"That's a pretty simple law," I murmured.

"Simple is usually better," Ningul said. "Most of the Council laws are fairly concise and direct."

"That could help us. Human laws are pages and pages of verbosity, and even then the lawmakers tend to overlook something obvious that can be exploited."

"How so? I don't understand what you mean," Fiona asked.

"Fewer words, more loopholes," I reasoned.

"I don't see how there are any loopholes for Fortuna and me. We are human, and we are residents of the circus," Mark disagreed.

"Well, here's one—you said any privately held property harboring residential humans is subject to forfeiture. What the paper actually says is any privately held property harboring residential humans *at the time of inquest* is subject to forfeiture. So, what's officially considered the time of inquest?"

Fiona shrugged. "I don't know. When they showed up here?"

"An inquest is usually a judicial inquiry," I pointed out. "They *asked* nothing when they showed up here. Just made threats and accusations, and there was no judge."

The inquest is what you delayed for seven days, Samson said.

"Okay, so Samson just said the inquiry is actually at the end of the seven days," I told the group. "Can't we just officially untether Fortuna and Mark on that day, and then move them back in the next day?"

Ningul shook his head. "At the risk of pointing out that's too easy, that's too easy."

"According to you all, it would also leave us helpless in the human world with a price on our heads from the witches," Fortuna said. "Not a position that I want to put myself in."

Mark agreed.

"See if they can hang out at the Makepeace Circus for a day?"

"Charlotte, you're just kicking the can down

the road," Fiona argued. "Even if we avoid consequences that day, they will be back. The wicked triplets don't give up that easily, and for some reason, they have it in for us."

"I still don't understand why. I mean, I'm barely a ringmaster and barely a witch, here. They didn't have it in for my uncle like this." Fiona sighed and caught me in a bear hug, crushing me until my sides ached. Releasing me just as rapidly, she banged her fist down on the parchment. With a deep breath, she continued calmly despite her emotional outburst.

"We'll find out at some point, Charlotte. For now, though, we need to focus on figuring out a way to avoid the catastrophe happening in less than a week."

CHAPTER 4

"YOU ARE THE RINGMASTER!" ANYA HOWLED, hovering over my bed. "Tell my sister that what she did is *unacceptable!*"

I stared through gritty eyes at the naiad. There was so much about the Magical Midway I had gotten used to. Always having people around you all the time. The smell of hay and sugar invading my nose. Constant lights flashing at the edge of my attention. I even came to love my yurt pie slice, a little corner of the management yurt I expanded and renovated with magic.

One thing still drove me nuts, and that was the lack of ways to lock a yurt.

"Mornin', Anya. I wondered where you were last night," I grumbled. "What's Alessandra done?"

I reached to the side table for the morning coffee Anya *surely* must have brought me. *Surely* she didn't barge in here at the crack of dawn to scream at me without a coffee offering. As my hand slammed over my water glass from the night before, I sighed.

"Not Alessandra. I have *her* under control at the moment. Alexa! Alexa has returned from the outside world, and you would not *believe* what she's done! It's abominable! Terrible! I can barely contain my fury!" Anya screeched and thumped her fists on the bed next to me.

"Same here," I told her. I moved to sit up.

"You know?"

"No, no, never mind. Continue with your righteous screed," I told her, swinging my flannel-encased legs over the side to the floor. Just as I leaned forward, Fortuna's head poked in.

"Everything okay in here?" the seer asked.

"No! My sister has abandoned everything we stand for! Everything!" Anya shouted at her. "Charlotte has to do something!"

"What did she do?" Fortuna asked me as she stepped in.

"I have no clue. I was just sleeping here."

"How can you sleep at a time like this?" Anya shook my arm.

"Well, clearly, I *can't*," I told her shrugging out of her grip. I looked at Fortuna and shrugged again. I was clueless. Anya couldn't seem to get past her indignation to explain what she was so indignant about. Fortuna walked over to our friend and rested a gentle hand on her forearm.

"Anya, *what* happened? Tell us, perhaps we can help."

"Oh, I *doubt* that. Though we *will* have front row seats to your execution since Alexa now has a *flat* in Imperatorial City!" Anya spat the word condo through her lips as if it were poison. "A *flat*! An *apartment*! When in the history of this orbiting rock has a naiad *ever* lived in Imperatorial City? In a condo, no less! *The building doesn't even have a pool!*"

Imperatorial City was the legislative seat of the entire paranormal world. I'd never been there myself, but I'd heard it was a lot like Manhattan. Well, if Manhattan was infused with magic and the city administrators were all flamboyant and fond of glitter. It was also a moderated city, much like the Magical Midway was a moderated traveling paranormal "town." No one could simply *move* to Imperatorial City, you had to petition for entrance and the right to call it home.

Rumor had it no one's petitions were granted

unless they brought something of value to the Witches Council. Imperatorial City was their seat of power, after all.

"What do you think she offered the Council?" I asked Anya.

My friend froze, and her face became tight. "What do you mean?"

"Surely you know the stories of *Impy*," Fortuna said, using Imperatorial City's slang nickname. "You have to get the approval of the Council to own real estate of any kind there, and for that, you offer them something in return."

"Or someone," I added, looking at Fortuna pointedly. Anya shook her head no, her eyes widening when she grasped our insinuation.

"Alexa wouldn't *do* that," she argued. "My sister may be flighty, stubborn, and stupid, but she would never work with the Witches Council. It goes against everything we believe in!"

"So does living in a condo in a witch city," I pointed out. "Or so you said. I don't know, Anya. The timing seems suspicious. I've never met Alexa in all my years of visiting here. Suddenly, she shows up? *This* week of all weeks?"

"Look, Charlotte, I like you, but we're talking about my sister. Tread *carefully*, ringmaster." Anya's eyes flashed with anger as her fingers flexed. My hotheaded friend had always been quick to explode, but the cold calmness with which she delivered her warning chilled me.

"You know her, Anya. I don't. You tell me. Why do *you* think she came back here?"

"To bring her sisters with her to Impy." Fiona sailed into the melodrama unfolding in my bedroom. My blond friend walked passed Anya and Fortuna to hand me an extra large *WakeyWakey* drink from Brownie's Brownies. It was so strong it didn't even have an innovative or flowery name. I grabbed the warm container and gulped. "Avalon told me about all the havering."

"All the what?"

"Havering," Fiona told me. "Havering, foolishness, silly talk."

"Is that a carnie term?"

"You know, you *have* some Scottish ancestry, witch. Would benefit ye to learn a thing or two."

"Weren't you *born* in New Jersey?" Fiona glared at me. "Never mind." Kelpies maintained a light Scottish accent and used slang and jargon none of us were familiar with. For what specific reason, I did not understand. Some things it was better not to ask about.

"At least I wasn't born in *Impy*," Fiona scoffed. Turning away from me, she confronted Anya.

"What did your hag of a sister do to get a fancy condo overlooking the Castle Sapience?"

Anya's biceps flexed and she glared at Fiona.

"Stop it, both of you. This isn't helping anyone—"

We need you, Samson broke into my mind mid-speech. I held up my hand to the two women and focused on my familiar.

I'm kind of busy at the moment. Fiona and Anya are about to come to blows here in my yurt.

Let them. We need you. Mark Botsworth is missing. Come to the Lion's Den at once before Serena eats me.

A quick check of my inner mental Magical Midway inhabitant roster confirmed that Mark Botsworth was no longer anywhere on the grounds. His tethered connection stretched far from this place.

Farther than a mortal being could have gotten alone.

"Everybody step off," I pointed at Anya. "Go get your sister, and meet us back here. If I'm not here, wait for me." Her faced flashed and mine hardened just as quickly. I stepped toward her. She nodded and stomped out of my yurt twice as hastily as she walked in.

I exhaled and turned to Fiona and Fortuna.

"Fiona, you help Anya. Fortuna, come with me. Mark Botsworth is missing."

Serena was in lioness form.

And she was *huge*.

When Serena and her clan performed in the circus, they were African lions. Beautiful, regal, and massive, but pretty much just an average-sized lion. If an averagely-sized lion could ever be *just* anything.

In her current form, Serena was a rare Asiatic lion—and not just Asiatic, one of the *exceptionally* huge and stocky and powerful ones. She had to be at least five hundred pounds, and her head was even with my shoulder. I didn't know whether her form was a choice or her natural form, but it was striking to behold.

Her stomach flexed as she repeatedly roared, pacing. The roar was unlike anything I had ever heard before, a *ga-urrrrr* that sounded almost like a demand or plea. Various citizens of the Magical Midway milled around well away from her, nevertheless they snuck fascinated, sympathetic glances.

"Serena," I said, stepping into the unofficial

circle that hemmed in the big angry cat. "Serena, I need to talk to you." The lioness turned and lowered her head to stare up at me with golden eyes.

I wouldn't step toward her if I were you, Samson sent me. *I remind you again that we are dreadfully short of ringmaster choices should you become lunch.*

She won't hurt me.

She will hurt everyone in this circus if she's angry enough, Sampson disagreed. *Someone has taken away her life-size cat toy, and she is decidedly put out about it. I wouldn't get within leaping distance if I were you.*

The big cat paced in a figure eight in front of me, her eyes never leaving my face. The thoughts I could read from her were nothing more than a jumbled haze of bright red anger and pain. Serena's head was remarkably snakelike as it laser-focused on me regardless of what position her body was in.

For once, could you listen? *I know you need to push the boundaries of what everyone tells you is possible, but I* am *a cat. The hairs on the back of* my *neck are standing up, and she's not even looking at* me. *Do not get closer!*

I hadn't been making any forward momentum, but out of an abundance of caution, I stepped back. A sense of smug satisfaction radiated from Samson's hiding place. "Serena, if you simply pace and roar, I can't talk to you about what happened. Can you please change back so I can talk to you? I need to find Mark. You need to help me do that."

Clancy O'Blaze stood across from me on the other side of the informal circle whispering with Krog Kobald. The leprechaun and the goblin leaned into one another as their eyes darted here and there. Lucius, the Roman guard, stood a few steps behind them with his spear at the ready, but taking no action to deal with anything he was observing.

"You will have to approach her," Fortuna told me.

"Samson warned me against that."

"Samson is 1/100 her size. I don't think house cats and lions play around that much. She'll bounce off you. Well, you may ricochet off her. Either way, though, your insides are safe." Fortuna pushed me forward.

Your friend has a big mouth, Samson grumbled.

Clancy and Krog turned around and walked away toward the back of the haunted house. Their little legs were practically running away from the scene.

"Oomph!"

That was the sound I made as I landed on my back. In the dirt. With a 500-pound cat slapping at my face.

Fortuna had been right. Though laying in the dirt and being pawed at and gnawed on by a ferocious lioness was not the most comfortable and dignified thing I had ever endured, it didn't hurt. Serena's unsheathed claws clanged against my skin when she raked her razor sharp nails down my impenetrable body.

Well, you look ridiculous, Samson chimed in.

You're not helping.

Many watched, I waited, and Serena pounded.

I don't know why I went with the human option of letting Serena just get it out of her system. Despite all the magic-wand-waving, finger-snapping-powers I had at my disposal, it seemed like the big cat was merely a woman overwhelmed. If her mate was really gone, Serena appeared entitled to a meltdown.

I laid on the ground, and let her exhaust herself while attacking me.

~

It seemed like hours, but I think Serena batted me around like a cat toy for only twenty minutes. With a final half-hearted chuff, she shimmered and shifted into the elegant woman I knew. After the fury of her beatdown, I expected to be confronted with a wailing, shrieking woman when she turned and prepared for calm-down round two.

I was not.

Kneeling in the dirt, she was silent and tense. Her eyes downcast, she waited for me to get up with a quiet expectation. There was no apology for the beating she had subjected me to, nor any plea for help in finding Mark. Just silent, self-contained anger behind a mask of feline indifference.

Cats, I swear.

Hey, now, Samson said. *What's that human saying about keeping your head when all about you are losing theirs? That's valuable expertise.*

She beat me for twenty minutes, so she didn't keep her head. Anyway, it's not a saying, it's part of a Rudyard Kipling poem. You know, the guy that wrote 'The Cat Who Walks By Himself'? Surely you've heard of it.

Silence.

Didn't like it?

The man and the dog were not *smarter than the cat,* Samson snapped. *That's a ridiculous fiction written by a man that knew his limitations and wanted to turn it into entertainment. He should have had more cats, like that Poe human. Or that Hemingway.* Those *were writers.*

Right.

"Serena, are you feeling better now? Can we talk?" The golden woman nodded once and launched up from her kneeling position. Pivoting, she glowered at the bystanders gathered and narrowed her eyes to stare at each one. One by one, the assembled busybodies shifted on their feet, then stepped away mumbling to one another.

"My pain will *not* serve as entertainment for these creatures any further." Once she was satisfied we were no longer serving as entertainment, she led me back to the tent behind the public lion enclosure. Fortuna and Samson followed.

Leo, the sole male werelion, sat on top of a crate in a cross-legged position at the back of the tent. "Tell her," Serena told him with a dismissive wave. "Tell her what you told me."

"Of course," he replied with a bored nod. "I came into this area, and Mark was resting right where I am sitting now. I headed back to our yurt village to get my mane conditioner—my fur has been dry the past few days, and it needs a deep conditioning. The mane fur is—"

"Leo, I appreciate the hair update, but can we get back to Mark?"

Leo stared at me, blinked, and then tossed his golden brown hair back with a huff. "Of course, ringmaster. I forget that your *kind* has no appreciation for the significance of those things important to the rest of us."

What the heck was that about?

A male werelion's mane is very important. The darker and more abundant and healthier it is, the more attractive a male lion is to a mate, the more feared he is as an opponent, Samson explained. *It's like telling one of your males you don't care about the size of his—*

Got it! I cut Samson off, choosing to believe he was about to say hands.

"In any case, when I returned, he was gone," Leo said. "Serena could not find her plaything."

"I object to your denigration of my mate, Leo," Serena told the male werelion.

"I object to your *plaything*, but that seems to have not troubled you in any meaningful capacity, Serena," Leo responded coolly.

Serena stared at him, but said nothing.

I looked around the tent, and nothing seemed out of place. The werelions were like all cats, scrupulously clean, and their private area lived up to their natures. The hay covering the dirt floor was clean, and not disturbed. The crates, cages, and hay bales were stacked neatly along the sides. There was little in the area to indicate any kind of scuffle.

In fact, there was almost nothing back here at all. No sink, no shower. I glanced over at Leo, and the bottle of fancy French conditioner sitting next to him on the crate. "Leo, where would you condition your mane?"

"We have a soaking pool behind this tent for the pride and the streak."

"Streak?" Leo stared at me and grimaced at my question. Then he rolled his eyes.

"A group of tigers. They're called a streak or an ambush. We don't allow the bears in our pool."

"Can you show me?"

Long pause as his golden eyes stared at me.

"If you insist," Leo sighed and hopped down from the crate. Walking across the tent, he snapped his fingers at Fortuna and me as if we were trained pets he wanted to follow him. This guy was getting on my last nerve with his haughty demeanor. "Surely you have seen it before. You *are*, after all, the ringmaster. Are you not?"

"Humor me."

"If you require," Leo mumbled. Serena followed us out of the exit, and as we stepped back into the sunlight, my jaw dropped.

The soaking pool was the size of a regulation basketball court. Rectangular in shape, it jutted up against the shimmering back wall of the Magical Midway itself. I stared off into the distance but saw nothing beyond the barrier other than trees.

"Did you come here the front way by the petting zoo or the back way around the roller coaster?"

"Why?" Leo asked me sharply.

"I want to know whether you saw the front or the back of the lion area as you approached," I told him, and he nodded. "If you came around the front, Mark likely left out of the back, and vice versa. Since you didn't see him, I mean."

"I came around the back way," Leo said and pointed toward the roller coaster.

Leo returning through the back way would mean he walked directly up to the soaking pool. I squinted in the sunlight and looked around.

There was a sitting area next to the water for relaxing in humanoid form. Next to that, a cabana I assumed held towels and things needed for a dip. I walked toward the cabana.

"Do you have any more need of me?" Leo asked as he refused to follow. "I have other things that I need to do, and this has already postponed my schedule *considerably* this morning."

"Is there anything else you can think of?"

"I can think of many things," Leo said. "None that I wish to speak of. Serena has heard all of my conclusions before."

"And dismissed them," Serena replied.

"I have done my duty," Leo bowed. "Both to the midway, and to my pride. I will not wish you well in your search for the human. Wherever he is, it is better for Serena that he remains there. It is assuredly better for the Magical Midway that he *never* return."

"You are a *miserable,* arrogant pride leader," Serena hissed. Fortuna moved to stand next to Serena and placed her arm around the indignant woman for comfort.

"Be that as it may," Leo shrugged. "No rule against that. Leadership bars seem to be set lower and lower these days, do they not?" The handsome man looked me up and down, then rolled his eyes. With another condescending bow, he strolled away without glancing back.

While Serena mumbled curses and growls, I held up my hand to Fortuna, who was about to get going, too. "Just wait," I told them both and walked again toward the cabana. Both followed me. "I want to check on something. I have a hunch. If I'm right, you may want to save up your ire and just spend it all at once."

Pulling back the cabana curtain, I discovered the bright pink bottles as soon as I peered inside. At least six bottles of Leo's particular fancy French conditioner were tucked into the rear shelf next to the locker.

"Why would he lie?" Serena asked, blinking in bewilderment.

"Maybe he's not as tough as he thinks he is, and he saw Mark taken but got panicked. Maybe he saw something, and he chose not to get involved because he loathes your and Mark's relationship," I mused. "Maybe he's just a dolt. I don't know. I only know he lied about why he left. *If* he left at all. Everything else is speculation at this point."

Fortuna fumed. "I will speculate my foot right up his—"

"No," Serena interjected. Fortuna and I turned

to the troubled lioness. "He is the official leader of our pride. I must talk to my sister, Selena, first. Leo must not learn that we believe he knows more. He could demand that the pride leave the Magical Midway, and all of us would be gone. I would never see Mark again…if there is even hope of that now."

"You and Selena would be more than welcome to stay without that jerk," I told her.

"We would not," she told me sadly. "A suspicion is not enough to defy the pride leader. Our world has *rules*, ringmaster, as yours does. There is no other male lion here to fight for the honor of our pride. If Leo demands we leave, we must go or face banishment for defying our pride leader. It is the most dishonorable thing a werelion can do. We would be shamed. Forever."

"That's awful!" Fortuna told her.

"Even so," Serena agreed.

"Okay, let's go talk to Selena," I told the two women. "And let's not tell Anya about this latest development, okay? She's got enough going on with her own sister, I don't need to give her a sexist male that she can take her fury out on."

"This *is* a deep enough pool," Fortuna pointed out. I glared at her, and she shrugged. "I'm just saying…"

CHAPTER 5

As Fortuna, Serena and I raced across the fairgrounds in search of Selena, I spotted my uncle chatting with Coston, the elfin leader. With a wave, he clapped his hands together and made a beeline toward the three of us. His usually smiling face was veiled by a frown.

"Did you tell your uncle that Mark was missing?" Fortuna asked me.

"I've been a *little* busy," I told her.

"Maybe you should go talk to him. You know, without us around," Fortuna said, clutching Serena's arm. "I can go with Serena to find Selena. We'll all meet you back at your yurt when you're done talking to Phil."

"I'm sure getting my uncle up to speed won't

take *that* long," I asserted. Fortuna glanced back at uncle Phil and examined him as he grew closer. Turning back, her right eyebrow raised nearly off her had.

"I think you may be wrong about that. I recognize that look. We'll meet you back at the yurt," Fortuna said hurrying Serena away. After putting a few steps of distance between us, she swung back for a moment and looked me in the eye. "Stay cool, and good luck."

I thought about biting back a snide comment, but I didn't have time. I loved my uncle, but I was becoming frustrated at being handled like the puppet ringmaster of the Magical Midway.

I had a lot of empathy for my uncle. I really did. I mean, it's difficult to die and then become a phantom and then come back to life when someone else was chosen for your job. I realized that.

The look on my uncle's chubby face, though, made me feel like a little girl about to be given a chiding for not telling the adult in the room about an issue. The trouble was that I was supposed to be the adult in the room. I was assumed to be the Magical Midway's ringmaster.

Not supposed to be.

I *was* the ringmaster.

I would like to point out that if you let your uncle run everything and run over you—which, I'm not precisely saying you are—but were you doing so, you would have no one to blame but yourself if he assumes that you should defer to him. Things we do without thinking and for good reasons sometimes wind up becoming entrenched.

Shut up, Samson.

Whatever you are about to say, I would suggest that you not say it out here in public. We have enough drama going on at this circus to add another three rings. No one here should see the two of you fighting openly. Not now.

"What is going on with Mark?" Uncle Phil barked at me as he rushed up to Samson and me.

"Let's go to my yurt," I told him as I walked. "Fortuna and Serena will meet us there with her sister. I can catch you up."

"Talk," Uncle Phil said, crossing his arms and not moving.

Not here, I thought to him sharply. *Everyone is nervous, and you and I having this conversation in the middle of the midway will not help that. Please follow me back to my place so we can talk about what's going on.*

People walking by had already looked at us with concern. Since few people had psychic ability here besides Samson, my uncle, and I, I never got to see other telepathic folks converse with each other through their thoughts. Fortuna and Mark could do it, but they were practiced at keeping their faces from animating with each word they felt.

My uncle and I looked at each other as if we were about to throw down, waggling our eyebrows for punctuation on sentences no one could overhear.

Fine, Uncle Phil thought as he trudged back toward my yurt. *But as soon as we're in private, you and I will have a talk.*

Oh, goody, Samson thought. *I can't tell you both how exciting it is to have two ringmasters to juggle.*

As soon as we were within my brightly colored yurt, Uncle Phil sat down like he owned the joint and crossed his arms. "Well? Are you going to tell me now?"

"I will. First, I think I need to get something off my chest."

"*Now* you need to get something off your chest?" Uncle Phil stared at me with a look of doubtful curiosity. A satirical smile danced across his lips as he tugged on his mustache. "You think this is the right moment for a niece-uncle heart to heart? With Mark gone, your parents in danger, whiffs of a traitorous spy, and the Witches Council at the gate waiting to pounce? Absolutely, Charlotte. Let's chat about your feelings."

"You know, my Dad always said you were stubborn and wouldn't listen," I told him, barely containing my anger. "I'm getting what he meant. And I didn't say it was about my feelings. You don't even know what I was going to say."

Except it was about my feelings, and now he made me feel stupid for bringing it up.

"I'm listening."

"You're tapping your foot impatiently and glaring at me with a look that tells me you have exactly zero intention of listening to what I have to say."

We stared at one another in silence while Samson stood at my feet, washing himself.

"Charlotte, I have followed you here so you can tell me whatever it is you need to tell me. I suggest you get to it, because I am losing patience."

"Why did you take the whole thing back over?" I whimpered, cringing at my voice's pathetic timber. "You came back to some version of life, and now you're just stepping right over me. Everyone treats you like the ringmaster because you act like it. And now, in the middle of a crisis, you don't even trust me to handle it. I could tell just by the look on your face when you asked about Mark."

"I already know what happened to Mark," my uncle told me as he leaned forward. His voice had softened, and his eyes looked at me kindly even though his body was still tense. "I already know, roughly, what happened to Mark, about Serena's feline breakdown in front of many of our families. I know about Alexa's condo in Impy, and Anya's apprehensions. You may know more *details* than I, but I know plenty of it. Do you know how?"

I shook my head.

"Because I talk to everyone at the Magical Midway, Charlotte, and they talk to me."

"I talk to people."

"I *talk* to all, dear girl. You talk to your companions, and you wave to those that you pass, but you have yet to *truly* talk to everyone. Without communicating with everyone, without integrating yourself into their lives, without forming relationships, you won't always know what's happening and what needs to be done."

I wanted to argue with Uncle Phil and his observations, but I knew he was right. I'd always been an introvert. I didn't know if it stemmed from the fact that I could read everyone's true feelings, or if I just needed more solitude than everyone else. Whatever it was, I could be friendly enough, but I wasn't outgoing. I needed a reason to talk to people, and if I didn't have one, I didn't do it. I wasn't good at just reaching out for the sake of it.

"I'm not you, Uncle Phil. I just don't do that well."

"And so then you'll need more time. You're new to the family even though you have been one of us all along. You'll get there, Charlotte. I promise you will. Until then, though, please understand I care too much about this place to leave these people feeling uncared for."

Ouch. That hurt.

"I don't want anyone to feel like I don't care about them. Honestly, I didn't realize that's what I was doing." I walked across the room and collapsed in my favorite chair. "I feel like as soon as I get the hang of something, another thing just blows up that I'm doing wrong."

"Look here now," Uncle Phil said. "You have some fine talents. You bring a different perspective to this place, and you understand the human world better than any of us. Well, except the actual humans, perhaps. You have made friends—Anya, Avalon…you befriended them on your own."

"That was really a side-effect of the whole Dergal affair." Anya's sister was in a terrible relationship with the centaur that accidentally murdered my uncle. She was an incredible help as we tried to figure out what was going on, and by the end of the situation, she and I were friends.

"It was, wasn't it…" Uncle Phil twirled his mustache and looked up at the ceiling. "Perhaps that's how we get you to get out and about. You could serve as the Justice of the Peace."

"You want me to marry people?"

"I think you could be the Magical Midway lawgiver. It's not a position we've had for many years, but we're much larger than we used to be with so many other circuses gone. There is a precedent for it. You would head up the lares team, head any inquiries, and enforce justice when it was called for."

"You want me to be Judge, Jury, and Executioner?"

"Detective, Police Chief, Lawyer, Judge, Jury, and Executioner. Yes." Uncle Phil smirked.

"That's *preposterous.*"

"Our laws *are* old laws, Charlotte. Like I said, there is a precedent for it. And we're relatively small even though we are larger than before. We don't need six different people to do those jobs. Just one gifted person who's intent on hearing all sides, getting to know the issues, and determining what needs to be done."

This will mark you as a leader, and not your uncle's supply closet, Samson pointed out. *You've been critical of the Romans and how they run security since you got here, too.*

"That's because there's been a homicide, an execution, and a kidnapping since I got here."

Don't forget about the attack from the Witches Council.

Uncle Phil cleared his throat and shot Samson a look. "Speaking of the Witches Council, this would put some conventional rules between them and us, at least a bit. This is a formal legal position, Charlotte. It would allow us some defenses, some respect. Presuming, of course, we get out of this latest scuffle."

"Okaaay," I drawled. "Let's try it. Is there a

book or something on how I do this? What the job entails and all that?"

Uncle Phil shook his head no. *Of course not.*

"Fabulous."

"Here," Uncle Phil reached into his pocket and handed me a ring. "Put this on, and it's a done deal." I reached forward and studied the small gold ring. It was plain, didn't glow, and didn't vibrate, so I shrugged and placed it on my finger. Bracing, I waited for lightning to strike or wind to whip around me to stamp my newfound elevation, but nothing. Not so much as a paranormal murmur or a tiny wind gust.

"Well, that was anticlimactic."

"Not everything has to be vivid and dramatic, Charlotte," Uncle Phil said. "Now, go forth, and law-give!"

"Um. Right."

All hail the lawgiver, Samson replied.

Oh, shut up, cat.

I heard that.

The Atwater sisters rushed into my yurt like a storm only three naiad sisters could produce. Skin headed Anya, shy Alessandra, and furious Alexa plopped down on my sofa. Anya and Alessandra's arms crossed while Alexa crossed her legs, bounced her high heel and stared at me with empty eyes. Lucius Larry stayed in the doorway watching while my uncle explained to him I had made myself the official Lawgiver of Magical Midway.

"Boss?" Lucius asked Uncle Phil, perplexed. Uncle Phil shook his head no and pointed to me. "Boss?" Lucius asked in shock, pointing at me. My uncle nodded.

"You know, Lucius, I've been your boss for three months now, so this really shouldn't come as such a shock." I crossed my arms, too. If everyone else would be snippy and defensive, I may as well join in.

"Sir," Lucius slammed his fist across his chest with a clank and bowed his severe Roman head, sinking his chin to his chest.

"Please don't do that," I stammered. He replayed the entire thing over again.

In a lot of ways, I don't think my uncle's idea of my being the lawgiver was an honor. How on earth was I going to manage a security force of five when four members never said more than one word at a time? "Lucius, can you go get your brother Bob? Let's have him deal with this in here, okay?"

Bob may talk like a guy on a perpetual vision quest, but at least I could carry on a conversation with him. Lucius clanked his chest again and bowed. Then he pivoted and marched out the door.

"Alexa. It's nice to meet you. My name is Charlotte Astley, you may have heard of me?" I approached Alexa and held out my hand. "It's such an honor to meet Anya and Alessandra's sister. I've heard so much about you."

The naiad sisters all had mysterious beauty, even the rough-and-tumble Anya. Their features were perfectly symmetrical and intensely exotic. Each sister had a particular type of beauty. Anya was a lovely wild thing with rough edges, Alessandra was delicate and gentle like a flower. Alexa was…

Alexa was innocence twisted. Her beauty was sharp, like a knife, but exaggerated and covered with layers of glitter and makeup. Too much paint, too much hairspray, and heels far too high to be parading around a circus. Alexa exuded impatience, continuing to shake her leg, adding the monotonous tap of her razor-like fingernails against my side table.

Her impolite response to my open hand, I suppose.

"Have I offended you?" I dropped my hands, but remain standing in front of her, smiling.

"Everything about you offends me," Alexa told me. "I don't see what my invitation to my sisters has to do with *you*."

"A member of the circus disappeared today," I told Alexa, sitting down in the chair beside her. "Since you just came from Impy, I thought you might know something that could help us find him. Just last night the Witches Council came here and threatened us if we didn't hand over Mark, the man who's missing, and another member of the circus."

"So?"

"So, it just seems like a lot of coincidences for one night, you know? You returning, their threats, Mark disappearing," I reached out and placed my hand on her knee.

Since I sat down, I had been trying to read Alexa's emotions or thoughts. I was getting nothing off the naiad. It was as if she was wrapped in a protective shield. Any attempt I made bounced off her.

"This is the circus." Alexa waved her arms around. "*Nothing* at this place is a coincidence."

She is shielded, Samson told me. *That's why you cannot read her. She is encased in a shield to prevent anyone from reading her or influencing her.*

Is that something naiads can do? Shield from me?

Not naturally, no. If I had to make an educated guess and, let's face it, I am the most educated on these fairgrounds, I would say someone placed protection around her before she came back here.

"Perhaps you're right, and there are no coincidences. Is there something you want to tell me?"

"*Me,* Lawgiver?" Alexa laughed as Anya whacked her. "I have nothing to tell *you* at all. I'm not even significant enough to be relaxing in your private quarters. I don't know why you yanked my sisters and me into this—"

"I asked her to talk some sense into you!" Anya shouted.

"I have more sense than you two," Alexa spat and whirled on her sisters. "You run a boat ride for snotty, ungrateful humans! We are naiads! We bring humans to their death as a sanction for their sins! We don't help people play kissy face on the love boat ride!"

"Alessandra and I like our lives." Anya stood up. "We do as our parents did and their parents before them! Mother would drown you in a lake if she knew that you had a condo in Impy. And what did you *give* them for that condo?"

"Yes, water spirit, what did you trade them for your luxury?" Serena asked, followed by her identical sister Selena, Fortuna, and Fiona. Samson's fur spiked out as he made his way behind me. "If you traded my mate for your riches, if I find out you had anything to do with his loss, I will peel the—"

"Folks, I understand that everybody is upset, and everyone is concerned, but we don't attack each other, all right?"

"All right, all right, lawgiver boss type lady!" Bob shouted across the room as he shoved his way in through the yurt opening. "We got ourselves a lawgiver now, folks, and that means stuff just got real! Yo-yo, baby! It's *lawgiver* time!"

Bob ran in place to a beat that only he could hear. The assembled group was silent as the jovial Roman danced and hooted. Bob gave a few more shouts as he jumped up and down and clapped his hands. "Lawgiver time, baby!"

"Are you *done*?" I asked him.

"Wait." He clapped twice more, crossed his legs, and spun around twice. "Now, I think I'm done. Sorry, boss, but this is an exciting day! A lawgiver position hasn't been occupied for 150 years! This is like living history, man!"

"You're the *lawgiver* now?" Fiona stared at me.

"Uncle Phil and I talked about it and thought it would be a great way for me to talk to more people at the Magical Midway. You know, really get out more."

"Well, it will do *that*," Fiona responded and raised her eyebrow.

"What?"

"Did your uncle tell you about the once a week courts you have to hold?" Uncle Phil jumped up and waved his hands in a cutting motion toward Fiona while shaking his head no.

"The what?"

"How about the reports to the Witches Council? Interfacing with human law enforcement?" she asked as Uncle Phil continued to hop up and down like a lunatic. I shook my head no. Uncle Phil glared at Fiona. Fiona smiled at him and held up her hands.

"You have a big mouth, Fiona. I didn't want to overwhelm her. She'll do just fine. Right now we need to concentrate on getting Mark back. Once the current crisis has passed, I'll go over everything she needs to do," Uncle Phil told my friend.

My friend was covering up her mouth so I wouldn't see she was laughing at me.

"Okay, lawgiver, whaddya got, then?" Alexa laughed. Anya frowned.

I exhaled.

CHAPTER 6

OPENING MY EYES TWO DAYS AFTER THE WITCHES Council threat and one day after Mark disappeared, the sunlight spilling through my canvas windows seemed more like a spotlight than a greeting. I hadn't figured out how to defeat the witches, or who was responsible for Mark's apparent kidnapping.

I glanced over toward my pull-out couch and spotted Fortuna sleeping peacefully with her arm draped around a baseball bat. Despite all of the paranormal solutions at our disposal, Fortuna went back to the essentials.

Only five days left, Samson said as he licked my forehead, spewing out and hacking my long hair.

Why do you do that?

Do what?

Lick my hair? You know it's long, you know you will hack on it. You keep doing it, though.

I do, don't I? Samson agreed as he pulled his head back and pulled his face from side to side to dislodge the strands stuck in his teeth. *I suppose I'm grooming you. Though it would take me hours to make you presentable.*

Thanks. I sat up and glanced at the clock. Ten a.m.? I slept way, way too long. I rarely slept beyond eight in the morning anymore. The sounds of the circus started early, and it was impossible to shut off the noise without using some kind of magical shield. I was too worried that I would miss something important to go that far.

"Morning," Fortuna mumbled.

"How'd you sleep?"

"If you could ringmaster this into a real bed for the next few days, I would appreciate it." The seer stretched and grumbled as her muscles creaked. "If I am going to be executed for running away to the circus, I would prefer to die after having a pleasant night's sleep."

"Don't even joke about that," I told her and

threw a pillow in her general direction. "That's not funny."

"I wasn't trying to be funny." Fortuna sat up. Her eyes were puffy as if she had been crying, and her morning voice was coarse and rough. "I'm well aware of the situation I am in, Charlotte. I am doing the best I can to accept it."

"Well, don't. We're going to find a way around this. I will not let anything happen to you, Fortuna."

"I admire your certainty." Fortuna's head bowed, and she placed her hands over her head, mumbling something into her knees.

"What? I didn't hear that."

"I am used to this, Charlotte," she said, raising her tear-stained face. "I didn't have my talent the way I have it now, but I always…knew things. My family was always frightened of me. I didn't look like them or talk like them. I was adopted at birth, did you know?"

I shook my head no.

"I was. I was a short, dark-haired, nerdy, curvy girl with thick curls adopted into a family of tall, athletic and outgoing blonds. You never had to work to detect *me* in family pictures," she laughed. "I always stood out. They tried to love me, but I was always peculiar. They never understood me. And when I got flashes of future vision, little tiny tendrils of my talent poking through...well, then they were afraid of me."

"Fortuna, I'm so sorry."

"That's not even my real name. Well, maybe it is. My adoptive family called me Heather. Heather Anne Addington. I mean, can you picture it? Me? Heather Anne Addington?"

I couldn't picture it. In my mind, Heather Anne Addington was a blond girl living in an estate. I could see her in a delicate tennis outfit, blond hair shining. Trying to place the name on the short, curvy gypsy woman in front of me didn't quite fit.

"I chose Fortuna Delphi. Delphi for the Delphic oracles, the Pythia. Fortuna for the Goddess of Fortune. I hoped that by taking her name, maybe she would make a little luck for me when I left home. And it worked, too. Within two weeks, I found the Langdon circus. Everything became clear, and I knew what I was and where I belonged."

"And now, it's like you don't belong all over again," Fiona whispered from the door. Fortuna turned, startled, and then nodded.

"My family just didn't accept me, though. The paranormal world wants to *kill* me."

"We're the paranormal world, too, Fortuna," Fiona told her. "Those intolerant women with their bigoted views are not the paranormal world, as much as they would like to think they are. Heck, they're not even the entire Witches Council."

"I know that," she acknowledged. "It's hard to remember they are just three witches. The other ten witches on the Council are not known to be so…angry."

Fiona rolled her eyes. "They're not known for much of anything other than relaxing in their palace. Flighty women that do not understand what happens in the real world. Paranormal or otherwise."

"You don't think the rest of the Witches Council knows what Mina, Mabel, and Mercy are doing?" Fortuna and Fiona both shook their heads no. "How could they not know?"

"Everyone knows the other ten witches inherited their places and rubber stamp whatever the wicked triplets dictate they should. Doing otherwise would require far too much work." Fiona plopped down on the bed. "They hardly come out unless it's Council Day. And on Council Day, they flutter around and wave from their patio like they were all the Queens of England."

"They're all women?"

Fortuna looked astonished. "Of course they are. Men can't have leadership positions in witch councils. Or towns."

"But my uncle was the ringmaster. And Roland Makepeace is the ringmaster of Makepeace Circus."

"Why do you think they hate circuses so much?" Fiona asked. "Well, that's not the only reason. But it is certainly one of the many reasons they think we're some crazy outsider group that refuses to follow the rules."

"The rules are stupid. And sexist." Fiona shrugged. "Doesn't anyone else feel that way?"

"It wouldn't matter if they *did*," Fortuna pointed out. "The paranormal world is not a democracy. If people felt that way, what could they do about it?"

"I refuse to believe things just are the way they are, and nothing can be done about any of it."

"That's why we love you, Charlotte." Fiona threw her arm around me and gave me a smack on the cheek. "And if you could expand the Magical Midway so it would encompass the entire world, you could fix everything."

It was incredible that with all the magic at their disposal, the paranormal world was facing some of the same problems as the human world. Even more, in a way. The people here were ruled by dictators that got away with abuses because of ineffectual leadership. The more things change.

"So, what do we do?" Fortuna asked.

"Right now, the answer is defeating the three witches on this issue," I told her, hopping out of bed. "After we save you and Mark, we'll worry about taking over the paranormal world and starting a mutiny."

"They're usually here," Arden told me as he rubbed the dime pitch game board. "I dunno where he and Krog went. They been gossipin' and huddlin' all the time lately. Dunno what's with those two. Clancy's chapping my green buttocks, I'll tell you."

"Your rear is green?" I asked the grumpy leprechaun.

"What?" He peeked up at me, insulted. "My bum's lily white and soft as a baby's, I'll have you know. Maybe you want to find out sometime, eh, Charlotte?" Arden wiggled his unruly red eyebrows up and down in what I presumed was an attempt at seduction. Instead, it reminded me of being aggressively threatened by bright orange caterpillars. "'Sides, I always wanted to kiss me a lawgiver. Very sexy, that. What you want Clancy for, anyhow?"

"Yesterday when Serena was having a fit, I saw Krog and Clancy run off when I arrived. Since they were near the lion area, I wanted to find out if they'd seen Mark. Or anyone around that area that shouldn't be."

"Dunno what the two of them would do over there. I wouldn't think those two would hang between the werewolves and the lions for leisure, if you know what I mean."

"Not sure I do."

"The shifters keep to themselves mostly," Fiona told me.

"You mean us short creatures keep away from you shifters," Arden corrected.

"I'm not a shifter," Fiona snapped.

"You walk like a human. You change into a filly. That's shifter enough for me, eh?"

"Arden," I said, stepping in front of Fiona. "Your booth is right next to Mark's tent. Did you hear anything, see anything unusual? Maybe you overheard a quarrel or saw someone the morning he disappeared that struck you as odd?"

"Ever since he and that lion started their

tomfoolery Mark hasn't been around his tent all that much," Arden said, stepping back and staring at the board. He squinted, leaned forward, and scoured a corner. Nodding to himself, he turned back. "Just when the fair is open. Once the humans all leave, he goes somewhere. Between you and me, I think he's been trying to avoid that Leo."

"Why's that?"

"Have you met him? What a pretentious sod that youngster is. If you talked to him over five minutes, you'd avoid him as much as you could, too. Ugh. There he is now."

Leo walked with his back erect, head held high, between the haunted house and Mark's silent tent. All he needed was a spotlight and some background music and his manner would have been perfect for a Paris runway. As he passed us, he flashed a smile that seemed more like a sneer.

"Charming," I murmured as he walked away.

"I don't see the big deal with people dating whoever they want. If I met a sexy lioness that liked 'em short and crass, I'd give it a go, too. Leo did not feel the same way about Mark and Serena."

"Why do you think that?"

"Was hard not to hear them arguing when Serena first dated Mark," Arden said as he sat down on his stool, took out his pipe, and sucked air through it. "Seems that when he became the head of the pride, he assumed Serena would be his."

"Why's that?" Fiona asked.

"Her father was the old pride leader."

"Why would that mean she would become his girlfriend or wife or whatever?"

"Because he decided. Least, that's what it seemed like. Since there are only three werelions, in his mind, it was her or her sister. He decided he wanted Serena, and she decided he didn't get to decide for her."

"I would think not," Fiona agreed.

"Did you ever see Leo talking with Alexa Atwater?"

"Is that girl back? Oh, lordy me." Arden threw back his head and laughed. "If she's back, Acadia can't be too far behind. Though let's hope not."

"Who's Acadia?" I asked, confused.

"The fourth and final naiad sister. Anya, Alessandra, Alexa, and Acadia Atwater. Anya and Alessandra are official residents here. Acadia and Alexa are not, but they visit annually. Usually not at the same time, but

Arden's right." Fiona scratched her head, shrugged, and sighed. "If Alexa is here and there's trouble, Acadia is no doubt going to show up."

"We still don't know why Alexa is here," I pointed out.

"Really?" Arden asked. "That girl's been trouble since she crawled out of the river with her fully formed attitude. I'd lay money on Alexa having something to do with Mark disappearing."

"Why's that?"

"That girl's always been trouble. Always been. Always will be. Heck, talk to Bolt over at Sticky Walls. He'll tell ya all abut her."

The ride looked like a big jewel. Sticky Walls sat across from the haunted house, and as we walked by I saw little Anna's glowing face in the window. She waved, and then her face fell as she looked right and left. As soon as she was satisfied no one would catch her peeking, she hopped up and down and waved again. I waved back and grinned.

"That seems so odd," I told Fiona.

"What?"

"That a child ghost just remains a child. Forever."

"It's not necessarily permanent," Fiona said and she waved at Anna. "Some people die, and they're not all that disturbed by it. They get up, dust themselves off, and move on to wherever they are expected to go. With some souls, it's different. They need more time to prepare, to heal."

"Yeah, but hundreds of years? That's a lot of time to be a child."

"Look around you, Charlotte," Fiona said. She pointed in a circle around her head. "We exist and survive because humans want to play like they're children. We are where beasts are friendly, shocks are safe, risks are harmless, and ample amounts of sugar don't make you gain weight or rot your teeth."

"Is that true? About the sugar?"

"No, but the humans eat here like it is," Fiona pushed passed the Sticky Walls gate and stuck her head into the open side door. "Anyone in here?"

"One second!" A deep male voice echoed from within the ride. Deep clangs, chimes, and crashes followed. Then a string of hissing and profanity (I assumed) in a language I didn't recognize. "One second more!" A big boom from within the bowels of the silver and red beast shook the platform we stood on.

"My apologies, ladies," a tall, lean man said as he stepped out of the shadows. "The old girl's been acting up when we put it on super sticky mode." I had seen Bolt from far away, but that view did not prepare me for how striking he was. Up close, I could see the man's eyes were ice blue, almost crystalline, and his skin was the palest white I had ever seen on an individual before.

"Charlotte, have you met Bolt?"

"We've said hi and acknowledged one another, but not really formally, no."

"I've noticed our new ringmaster spends most of her time with her girl gang," Bolt told Fiona as he glanced at me. "Unless you are a member of that gang or the Makepeace Circus, it seems getting time with her is a bit of a challenge. Luckily, we have a spare ringmaster that is a bit less aloof."

Bolt's tone did not seem accusatory or cruel, and yet his words stung me. Uncle Phil was right, and he was not the only one that noticed. "I'm not aloof by nature," I told him. "I think I've just grown up not having a wide variety of close friends. I have to learn to be a member of a big, close-knit family like this."

"Big and family? That I will grant you," Bolt laughed as he grabbed a towel and scrubbed the sweat from his hair. "Close-knit? I may challenge you on that observation, Ringmaster. We have our pockets and cliques like any other group. Only *you* are expected to ignore all that. The rest of us? We keep in our paths, and work to overlook that which bothers us."

"Would you mind telling Charlotte what you overlook about Alexa when she's here?"

The friendly smile that had taken up residence on the elf's face dropped, and his eyes clouded with pain. Looking down the midway, his eyes searched for something. After a moment, he nodded. "Please, come inside. It's cooler in there, and I have a bottle of mead we can share. I think I need cool darkness as well as the mead for this conversation."

We followed Bolt into the thick darkness of the ride. Multi-color lights flickered on and off as if it was a disco. Bolt leaned to the right of the door and pushed a few buttons. The automatic door closed and the multi-color lights stopped their dancing. With a final button push, candlelight flared in the vast interior, bathing it in a gentle, otherworldly glow.

"Oh my gosh!" As I glanced around, the interior had been transformed from the ride to images of crystal mountains lining the circular room.

"This is just for us," Bolt said as he pulled out folding chairs. "Even if a human accidentally pushed the button, they could not see what we paranormals see in here."

"What is this place? Is it an image of something real?"

"Once it was real," Bolt said sadly as he gazed around. "Now, it is but a memory of a place that no longer exists, except in the hearts of those elves that remember. Perhaps one day I will share it with you. For now, I shall share my honey mead and tell you what you wish to know."

Bolt handed me a paper cup filled with a golden liquid. One sip and my insides felt as if they were coated with sunlight. Fiona accepted her cup, and Bolt smiled.

"Alexa and I loved one another. Or, at least, I thought we did," Bolt began as he sat back in his chair. "Have you met my ex-love yet?"

"Yes," I nodded. "Though if you don't mind me saying, it seems like you two are opposites." Bolt was elegant and spoke in a refined manner. Alexa struck me as crude, uncouth. I could not picture the two as a couple.

"What is that human world saying? Opposites attract?" I nodded. "As you have already surmised, we were opposite. I was excited by the wildness I found in her. She seemed comforted by the steadiness she found in me. Naiads are of the water, and very emotional. We elves are of air, and cerebral. We complemented one another. Or so I thought." Bolt sipped his mead, swallowing.

"They were together for two years," Fiona said. "Then Bolt asked her to marry him."

"Yes."

"Did she say yes?" I asked.

"She did. She seemed quite happy, too. Accepted the Vanda ring and wore it on the proper finger." Bolt spotted my confusion. "A Vanda ring is a pledge ring, much like a human engagement ring. Besides serving as the pledge to marry, it contains magical properties that make it quite valuable. Elves were often killed years ago before they could wed. To protect their betrothed, the ring could be moved upon a lover's death to a different finger, the word Vanda spoken, and all that the betrothed had would transfer to their love. It was our way of taking care of our intended in case of a tragedy."

"Uh oh," Fiona said.

Bolt shifted in his chair and blinked back tears from his icy eyes. "I was not aware that this could be done without the death of the one who gave the ring," Bolt confirmed tightly. "Alexa was informed when we traveled to Imperatorial City for her dress, by an unscrupulous witch that wished to buy it from her."

"She sold it?"

"No, Ringmaster. She made an agreement with the witch to divide the proceeds between them once she discovered the…riches of elves." The elf took a deep breath and exhaled loudly. "It was not something she knew, nor something I would have ever thought to tell her about. She did not return with me to the Magical Midway, and despite her sister's protestations, your uncle cast her out from this place for her betrayal."

"So, when you returned…"

"When I returned, I had no love, no money, and no hope for the future. Elves are quite serious about choosing a mate wisely. We have the magic to create one Vanda ring and one Vanda ring alone. I can never create one again, therefore I will be alone for the rest of my long life."

"Can't you get someone a regular engagement ring?"

"There are rules, Ringmaster," Bolt told me.

"I feel you people make up these rules just to make life more complicated for yourselves. You make one bad relationship decision, and you're cursed to be alone for the rest of your life? That seems like an out-sized penalty for picking the wrong girl to give a ring to."

"You may not have noticed yet, Ringmaster—"

"Please call me Charlotte."

"As you wish, Charlotte. You may not have noticed yet, since you are new to living in the paranormal world, but many of our consequences are quite severe."

"But, like, if you date someone, and then give her a diamond ring, what will happen? Will you explode into glitter confetti? Will she turn into a fish? You both will be cursed with the Ladyhawk thing where you are two different animals and can never be humanoid at the same time?"

"Well...no."

"Charlotte's a witch, but she didn't grow up in the witch world. She doesn't get some of these rules we have to live by," Fiona told him, and they nodded to each other.

"Now, hold on a second," I said, a little more sharply than I intended. "That's not it at all. What I'm saying is you guys are so conditioned to doing what you're told that it seems like no one stops and thinks about *why* you're doing what you're told. Whether you *have* to. I was trying to imply that if there's no consequence, you don't *have* to do it. You're *choosing* to."

Fiona and Bolt looked at me as if I'd grown another head.

"Have you guys never heard of democracy? Progress? Self-determination, even? How about freedom, liberty, and justice for all?"

"Those are *human* concepts," Bolt said.

"Maybe they should be *sentient being* concepts," I countered. "Not for nothing, but humans don't deal with this 'rules for no reason' stuff very well. Maybe you all could learn from the humans."

"Interesting observation coming from the all-powerful ringmaster," Fiona pointed out. "It must be easy to make that pronouncement when you are one of the most powerful magical beings on the planet. How's that view way up there on your high kelpie, your majesty?"

"Maybe it is," I agreed. "Would you rather I

approach this the way Roland Makepeace does? Or the wicked triplets? All fire and threats and dictates?" Bolt and Fiona laughed and shook their heads no. "So, next question—don't you think it would be better to *choose* between the three of us if you have to be ruled? Choose what type of person you want to lead? To make laws? To enforce them? To change them?"

"We couldn't choose our ringmaster," Fiona pointed out.

"That's my point. You couldn't. My question is why couldn't you do that? Why not choose a representative on the Witches Council? Or create a new, inclusive Council with representatives from all the clans? Why not? What's stopping any of these things from changing?"

Fiona and Bolt sat back and looked at one another in surprise as if the concept had never once occurred to either of them. I stood up.

"Thanks, Bolt, for your help. I will head back and meet up with my uncle. Maybe he knows something we don't that can help us with finding Mark." I looked down at the two troubled faces. "You guys, think about what I said. I know change is hard. The longer I'm here, though, the more I think it may be time for some things to change. At a minimum, Bolt, you shouldn't be condemned to live the rest of your life alone because you gave jewelry to the wrong someone."

The two nodded at me but didn't speak. I couldn't believe I'd rattled their brains that badly, but apparently I had.

Good.

CHAPTER 7

Can you meet me in my yurt? I thought out into the fairgrounds.

Who, me? Samson and my uncle answered simultaneously.

Yes, both of you. I waved again at little Anna with her spectral face pressed against the window, and she waved back. Her mother came next to her and tugged her away from the window gently, giving me a slight wave and a smile. Anna frowned, and her face faded from the window.

Hey, why don't the ghosts ever come out of the haunted house?

This is what you're concerned about now? Samson asked.

I saw Anna, and I realized she's always watching out the window, but she never comes out. She looks so sad sometimes. I glanced back once more at the huge decrepit-looking castle (that wasn't really decrepit) and wondered what it would be like to be stuck in its gloom all the time. It didn't seem like a great place for a little girl. Even one hundreds of years old.

The humans can see ghosts. Well, some humans can, Samson said as we connected with one another in front of the circus tent. The cat leaped to my shoulder and wrapped his tail around my neck. *One of your ancestors decided it was better not to risk them being seen.*

Is this necessary?

I didn't have any input on his judgment.

No, I mean this. I poked the cat in the rear on my shoulder. *You're not a parrot, Samson. Cats don't ride on people's shoulders.*

I fit fine. Besides, my legs are tired, and I just cleaned my fur. I don't want to get dirty again.

"Oh, for Heaven's sake." I stepped into my yurt and transferred the cat to the bed. He promptly climbed up to the top and curled up on my favorite pillow. Wonderful. "I swear, I don't know how you survived hundreds of years. You're so prissy about things sometimes."

I am faithful to my nature. I am a cat.

"Yeah, yeah, so you keep telling me."

"Good afternoon, my dears," Uncle Phil said as he scurried in. "I would love to report I have found Mark, and worked out our Witches Council issue. I would love to report those two things, but I cannot. Trying to thwart these diabolical plots is much harder without the ringmaster powers."

"Why? What would you do if you had them?" I asked Uncle Phil as I put a pot on for some tea.

"Well, first, I would follow Mark's tether thread to where he is so I could check on him. It would also help to identify his whereabouts. That might give us a clue regarding who helped make him disappear."

I clutched the edge of the table until my knuckles were white and breathed in and out. "You could do that as a ringmaster?" I asked without turning around.

"Of course!"

"So," I turned around, and pulled my face into the fakest smile I could achieve. I wasn't doing it to be coy. I read somewhere that if you smile, you can make yourself feel happy. And not livid. Or murderous. Both feelings I was trying to fight at that moment. "Since I have the ringmaster powers, does that mean *I* can follow Mark's tether and see if he is okay? And maybe see where he is?" I fluttered my eyelashes and smiled wider.

"Well, there's great risk associated with that, Charlotte," Uncle Phil said as he sat back in my delicate wicker chair. It creaked under the weight of him. "If you do it wrong, they'll see you. Then they'll know we know."

"They'll know we know what?"

"That Mark's been taken. And by who."

"So?"

"Well...we prefer to be invisible. We don't want them to know what we know and what we don't know."

"I get that. I'm asking why we don't want them to know what...oh, for goodness sake, why do we care whether they see me, Uncle Phil? Will I be in any danger? Can they hurt me?"

"No, it would simply be a visage of you if they even see anything at all. But they would know we know that Mark's gone." I stared at my uncle like he had grown another head.

"We *do* know that Mark's gone."

"Right. Then I don't see what the problem is, Charlotte. You're worrying about nothing, it would seem." Uncle Phil waved me off and coughed. My eyes narrowed as I glared at my uncle.

"Right, then, Uncle Phil. Why don't you explain what I have to do to find Mark, and I'll float off and check on him?"

"Absolutely, my girl," Uncle Phil grinned. "I think that's a wonderful idea. Let me go grab some things from my room. You should get one of the lares to hold guard, so we're not interrupted."

With the yurt entry sealed and Bob positioned outside to keep anyone from disturbing us, Uncle Phil threw fluffy pillows on my rugged floor. "It seems to be easier to do when you are as close to the land as you can be," he clarified as he grabbed a stone plate and placed it between the pillows.

"Why is that?"

"I have no idea." Uncle Phil grabbed a fire pot and set it on the stone. The fire pot looked archaic, darkened almost to solid black from the myriad of fires it must have contained over the years. "Many details about magic just are the way they are, Charlotte."

Who knew wielding magical superpowers

that could kill people would require such a zen, laid-back attitude? Throw caution to the wind, just accept things. Seems logical.

He didn't tell you not to take care, Samson said. *He is correct, though. There are things that even I do not understand. Not much, of course. In fact, very, very little. Now that I think about it, I know most things.*

Okay, why do I have to sit closer to the floor, genius?

That information is just trivia. It's beneath me to worry about such insignificant things.

You don't know, do you?

Silence from the all-knowing, all-seeing cat.

Uncle Phil gestured toward the fluffy pillows, and I sat down cross-legged before the contained flame gently flickering in the fire pot. Uncle Phil sat on the ground in front of me, and Samson hopped off the bed to sit next to the fire pot. "Clear your mind, Charlotte, of any worry or fear. Any concerns, any apprehension. Let all preoccupations just fall from your mind. Open yourself up to simply being one with the world. One with the Magical Midway. Focus on the fire."

My uncle's voice was calming, almost hypnotic, and he threw a blue powder onto the flame. With a deep breath, I tried to release all my worry and directly stare into the warmth and comfort of the small fire between us. "What is that odor?" I asked him. My voice sounded harsh, and far away.

"This is the scent of the blue rose, the rarest rose of all," Uncle Phil said as he tossed more blue powder onto the fire. "It joins us with the timeless energy of the earth and all of its beings."

"There are no blue roses," I murmured, but my voice sounded slightly drunk. A foggy haze of powder blue crept in the fringe of my vision.

"Hush now," Uncle Phil chided me. "Inhale in the scent of this magical flower, and it will help you on your spirit journey. Clear your mind, and continue to see the flame, and immerse yourself in the bouquet of the noble flower…"

With another deep intake of scented air, the blue haze closed in on my vision, washing the world in a patina of blue. As I breathed in and out, in and out, it closed its circled march around my perception until the flame in the center of my vision turned blue. With my next deep inhalation, the fire shot high into the air. Sparks flew.

"Remain calm, Charlotte," Uncle Phil said. "Just relax and do not fight what is about to happen."

Before I could pull myself out of the drunken

blue rose haze to ask my uncle what he meant, I felt the wafting smoke reach into me somehow. It was as if something was crawling within me, adding an extra layer to my skin, but *underneath my skin*. Despite the foreign feeling, I was not afraid, and it didn't make me nervous. As I felt the smoky invasion wrap itself around me, I cringed and closed my eyes as a loud pop startled me.

When I opened them again, the world was powder blue. It was shining with ethereal, gentle light. My head swiveled on my neck as I stared around the room, marveling at Uncle Phil's multicolored glow, and Samson's pure white shine. And my body...

Wait a minute.

How am I looking down at myself sitting cross-legged on the rug? I felt a flash of fear and leaned down to touch my head when Samson shouted *Stop!*

What the heck is this? How can I see this?

If you touch your body, you will rejoin it, and we will have to begin again.

"This is absolutely bizarre. Just bizarre." I stared down at my uncle, Samson, and my body. "Am I still alive?"

Of course you are. Some of your spirit remains to fasten you to your body, and secure the Magical

Midway to your bloodline. Most of you, however, has been divided from that physicality into traveling energy.

"I'm drooling," I told him.

Yes. There's not much of you left in there. Just sufficient to keep you breathing. So, regular body preservation, and the part of you that can magically defend yourself and the circus. Most of you is now floating up there.

Floating?

I looked down at my shimmering body and realized I was floating in midair cross-legged just to the right of the other version of myself. I extended my legs and panicked when I kicked them out toward the floor. "I can't get down!"

You can. Think that you wish to be on the ground and you will be there. You are energy, Charlotte. There is no gravity anymore, but you still have power over your spirit's mind. That mind controls your life form. Think up, down, stand. Your soul remembers your body. It will know what to do.

I thrashed in frustration and shouted within my head to go down. Whatever the sparkling spirit body was, it was first and foremost uncooperative. "I keep thinking down, but nothing is happening!"

Be calm, Charlotte. You can't order yourself to act.

You are willing yourself to be. Believe that you can stand. Know that you know how to do this, and merely assume that it will be done.

Despite having no lungs anymore, I breathed deeply in and out to calm myself. As I grew steadier, the heady scent of blue rose grew bolder. Despite, you know, not having a nose to smell anything. As my anxiety diminished, so did the spiritual representation of my body drift downward. I glided down and stopped. Though I didn't feel my feet hit the floor, I came to rest in a position that made it look as if I was standing.

Wonderful, Samson complimented me. *Now do the same thing, only this time focus your attention on your uncle and your desire for him to see you.*

Though I struggled a little bit at first, willing myself to be seen came much easier once I had mastered not floating in midair. Uncle Phil burst into a broad smile and clapped his hands with excitement.

"Wonderful! Your spirit is such a beautiful rainbow of colors, Charlotte!"

"Thanks, I think? Will that blue rose stuff pop anybody out of their body like this if they smell it?"

"No. This is a special capability of ringmasters. Well, and those of the bloodline.

Your father could do this if he wished. Your mother could not. Blue rose incense is very rare, and only those of noble blood can get it." Uncle Phil grinned and laughed again, pleased by my shimmering rainbow presence. "You are such a natural, dear girl."

While I, too, am pleased with how quickly Charlotte was able to master this, I would like to remind you both that the clock is ticking, and there is work to be done.

"Yes, yes, of course," Uncle Phil agreed and nodded. "Will yourself to see Mark's attachment, and then will yourself to follow it. If it's safe, you may wish to talk to him and make yourself visible to him the same way you've done with me. Then, when you are ready to return, simply will yourself back here."

If you get into trouble, you can call out 'rubberbandacon,' and you will crash back here into your body nearly instantaneously.

"Rubberbandacon? Not abracadabra or something fancier? More magical?"

"Are you criticizing our family's magical words? My magical words, in fact?" Uncle Phil frowned.

"Uh, no, Uncle Phil," I shook my head. "I didn't realize you had created this."

"I got myself into a little bit of a pickle a few years ago. A story for another time, dear girl. You must get going."

~

I nodded and willed to see the connection between Mark Botsworth and myself. A shimmering thread appeared in front of me reaching out to the west. The cord pulsed and shook, and it was taut with tension. Within seconds of willing myself to follow it, my world exploded into flashes of light. It was dark, but I could see everything outlined in a sheen of pulsing energy. I was in some kind of barn. Stacks of hay, crates strewn about, and stable-like enclosures. A horse shed, maybe? I could smell nothing other than the blue rose. From the back corner of the room, I heard whispered cursing and moved toward it.

"Mark?" I called, but there was no answer. Could he hear me? I wasn't sure if I had to will myself to be visible to every single person I came across, but I figured it couldn't hurt. I closed my eyes and calmed myself, willing Mark to see and hear me if he was in there.

"Mark?"

"Who's there?" someone asked sharply.

"Mark, it's me, Charlotte? Where are you?"

"Charlotte? Oh my gosh, Charlotte!" Chains rattled and clanked, and I heard him curse again under his breath. "I can't get up. Deo has me shackled. I'm in the back stall."

"Who's Deo?" I asked while I tried to walk toward him. After a few seconds, I realized that I wasn't closing the distance and just walked in place as if on a treadmill. Ugh. You must be kidding me. Squinting my eyes and focusing, I drifted toward, and then through the back stall. Mark yelped when I emerged. "Be quiet! They can't hear me, but they can hear you."

"Sorry! Sorry. I thought you were here, not… what are you? Oh no, are you *dead*?" Mark asked, looking despondent. His face was spattered with dirt, and his hair was matted with grass. Dried blood crusted against the right side of his skull just above his ear. Manacles attached to his wrists, and as he moved, I could see red where they had scraped him raw. "I am so sorry, Charlotte. I wish I could send messages to paranormals. I tried sending one to Fortuna, but I just wasn't strong enough. Please tell me your death wasn't my fault somehow."

"We must be too far away for her to have

heard you." I floated toward Mark and reached out to undo his manacles, but my hand simply passed through them and him. I couldn't manipulate anything. "And I'm not dead. I think I'm, like, astrally traveling here or something. At least most of me is. I would have been here sooner, but no one let me know I could do something like this. Where are we?"

"I don't know. I can't see out of that window up there, my chains won't stretch that far."

"Do you remember what happened?"

"I was hanging out in the lion area, and someone called, outside by the pool like they needed help. It sounded like they were behind the pool, so I looked to see." Mark yanked on his chains again and frowned. "A man was behind the pool all right, but he wasn't anyone I knew, and he wasn't inside the barrier. When I asked who he was, I was attacked from behind, and pushed into the man outside the boundary."

"Did you see who pushed you?" He shook his head no.

"I didn't see him. Or her. Whoever it was, they whacked me on the head but good, though. I think I was knocked out. When I woke up, I was here. Wherever here is."

Within a few days, the Witches Council would

return, and there was a mighty good chance that Mark would be taken by them, anyway. Why risk such a stunt just to get Mark out of the way early? Was it a diversion so I couldn't concentrate on the Witches Council issue? Or something else?

"Are you all right? I mean, are you seriously hurt?"

"This bump on my head isn't fun, but I'm okay. The guy that took me is feeding me, bringing me water."

"Have you seen anyone else?"

"No."

"Do you know who he is?"

"Someone called for a Deo, and he ran out of here like he was answering to that name," Mark said. "I don't know if that is his name, but I think it is. I know he's a lion shifter, and I think he's connected to our lion pride."

"Why do you think that?"

"He looks exactly like Leo, the head of Serena's pride at the Magical Midway. They could be twins." As Mark said Serena's name, he winced as though it was painful. "Is she okay? I hope she's not…Anyway, is Serena all right? They didn't do anything to her, did they?"

"She's a lot better than you," I told him. "Has

he said anything to you? Given you any reason this is happening? Asked you for anything?"

Again, Mark shook his head no.

"Okay, I need to find out where we are. I wish I could do something for you right now, but I don't have *hands*," I told him, holding up my see-through fingers and wiggling them. "Once I figure out where this is, we will come and get you. I promise. Will you be okay until I get back here?"

"Do I have an alternative?" Mark responded, smiling wearily.

"Man, I really wish you did. Okay, just…stay strong. We'll get you out. I promise."

Mark nodded. "Good luck, Ringmaster."

I sailed toward the wall behind Mark and went through it, out into the night.

CHAPTER 8

I don't know what I expected when I crossed through the wall and out into the night, but I could barely contain my shock when I realized I was at a circus. A centaur clopped down the path in front of me, and I felt sick when I understood there was only one circus this could be.

I was at the Makepeace Circus.

If the Magical Midway was an old-fashioned fair, the Makepeace Circus was an entirely modern carnival with the latest rides and a sleek, high-tech midway. Everywhere I looked, there were gleaming, brilliantly lit attractions and exquisitely constructed caravans, trailers, and houses. Humanoid staff in fresh, pressed uniforms walked hastily from one direction or another, looking intent on their tasks. A loud shout came from the west.

"Now calm down, everyone!"

I advanced toward the voice, drifting into the backyard of the Makepeace residential area. Log cabins surrounded a center clearing filled with picnic tables and benches. Dancing torch flames lit up the packed space as Roland Makepeace stood upon a stage and addressed the gathered throng.

"We have heard nothing from the Magical Midway or the Witches Council since they have been engaged in this latest brouhaha. I tell you, there is no reason to think this involves us at all." Behind Roland Makepeace, Gunther sat staring out over the crowd, his face tense.

"My cousin told me that someone stole one of their humans! Kidnapping? Now we can be plucked from the circus?" A large man with a handlebar mustache shouted at Roland. Standing up, the big man pointed at Gunther. "They will come for us next because of him!" Gunther flinched, but his gaze remained steady, and his head held high.

"Stop that! It is the Magical Midway's problem. It did not happen to us, and we have been assured by the Witches Council that despite their move against the Magical Midway, they will not move against us in the same way. We have nothing to do with what is taking place over there, for good or ill," Roland answered, waving off the man's concerns.

I discerned no deceit at all from Roland Makepeace. It seemed, though, that what he said was shaded by an overpowering desire to *believe* what he said was true. The ringmaster was unsettled.

Worried, profoundly, about Gunther.

"We are supposed to be *protected* here," a small woman called to him from the front. "Has that changed, Roland? We only put up with your garbage because we need your *shelter*. You assured us you had an arrangement with the Witches Council. That we were all safe here. If we are not protected, the bond is not worth the continual harping we put up with from you. And when they come for your half-breed offspring there, we may *all* be doomed!"

Half-breed?

I looked at Gunther as his face flamed hot and his eyes slid to the floor of the stage. Silence descended as Roland turned to glance at his son. As if he felt his father's eyes upon him, Gunther looked up. For a moment, the two men looked at one another. The younger man straightened himself in his chair, and the older man bowed. Turning slowly, he glared with a simmering fury at the cluster of angry people below him.

"Take care of your tongue, Meltanay," Roland told her as he struck his cane on the dais. The crowd murmured softly. "Recall who you are speaking to and deliver your next words thoughtfully. Whatever else he is, he is my son. Challenge me at your peril."

The small woman stood up. "The Witches Council was here and at the Magical Midway. Your 'heir' is partly human, and they are threatening the very survival of the Magical Midway based on *their* humans. This concerns us all, old man!" The woman raised her hand and jabbed it toward Gunther's father.

Holy unicorn horns.

Gunther was half-human. The shock of that revelation coursed through me as if I had a body.

"Get back to work! All of you! Now! Get out! Go!" Even in my unseen, intangible state, I started at Roland's furious explosion. He stomped and rumbled, brandishing his cane in the air as he shooed the members of the circus away. "Question me no more! You have pushed me to my limit! You are here at my pleasure and only that! Leave now before I exile you all! Or *worse!*"

Some scattered immediately, rushing away from Roland's howl. Others walked rapidly, but without a sense of panic. A few rolled their eyes and ambled away as if this was just another day and another explosion at the Makepeace Circus.

"Dad, you shouldn't—"

"*Shut* up, boy," Roland snapped at Gunther. "You are the *last* person I want to hear from at the moment. I warned you. I told you! Your obsession with that girl may very well have brought disaster down upon us all."

Father and son glared at one another, locked in silence. After a few moments, Roland turned aside from Gunther and marched down the stairs, retreating into the night.

Gunther sat on the stage alone. Seconds passed, then minutes. Gunther was…sad. Frustrated. Hopeless. If I had arms attached I would have run over and given him a hug.

"It's starting, you know. The prophecy."

The old woman that spoke was sitting in a chair at the center of the clearing, but I could have sworn everyone had left. Gunther looked up at her and smiled wistfully, acknowledging her.

"Maybe," he responded.

Wait—what prophecy?

"It is. You listen to old Ethel, boy. Tonight was marked. It is being witnessed even as we speak here now." The old woman stood up and shuffled toward Gunther. Halfway to the stage, she spun and stared straight at me.

I froze, afraid to breathe. It seemed that the old woman's eyes looked directly into mine. But that was ludicrous. Wasn't it? She smirked and dropped down her head in my direction, then shifted back toward Gunther. "It is the beginning."

"Of course it was witnessed. I bet the adjacent town heard my father yelling."

"They'll be here as the sun rises," she informed him.

"Who?"

"Don't be too upset at your father, Gunther. Everything is as it should be. You'll see."

"Ms. Elkins, you always make me feel better, but I never know why," Gunther told her, standing up and walking toward the edge of the stage. "I also never know what you're talking about." Gunther hopped off and walked toward the old woman.

"You will," Ms. Elkins cackled. "One half of you can sense it. The other half will come along soon. It is the prophecy of the Thirteenth Witch. It will change everything."

"Like I said, no idea what you're talking about. Can I help you back to your cabin?"

"Yes, yes, do that," she smiled and held out her elbow. Gunther took it gently, and the pair walked toward where I hovered. Invisible.

I hoped.

Ms. Elkins' clear eyes looked at me again as the two shuffled slowly, and I *could not* look away. I *knew* the old woman saw me, and I knew the fact that she could was dangerous. It should frighten me. Though it didn't.

"We should hurry on now," she said, nodding at me. "Nothing more to find out here, eh? We all need to get home, and then we all need to come back. Like a rubber band, we bounce and bounce, push and pull, hmmm?" The old woman laughed.

What the heck? I closed my eyes and rubber-banded back to my circus. Despite having found Mark and gotten a few clues, I was more mystified about what was going on than when I arrived. One thing rang in my head repeatedly above all else, though.

Gunther is half-human.

~

It was daybreak when I returned to the Magical Midway, and the usual suspects gathered to hear my report of what I found. My body was ravenous, and I jammed my face full of a sandwich while I revealed all I had learned.

Serena was reassured about Mark, but the group was dumbfounded to learn Gunther's origins.

"Okay, wait a minute, back up. Are half-human half-witch children that unheard of? I can't believe in the history of the paranormal world that cross-creature pairings are *that* out of the ordinary."

"Your people, Charlotte, are a cluster of creaturist, elitist *jerks*. It's happened in the past. There's a reason so many humans run around outside paranormal towns waving crystals at the sun and flipping over tarot cards," Fiona said. "But a paranormal that falls in love with a human *can't* remain in a paranormal town. They take off, they live as humans. Eventually, they forget. The Witches Council doesn't pay attention too much because they just…go elsewhere."

"They go away because the Council makes it too difficult for them to stay," Serena pointed out.

"The problem solves itself with their absence because there is an absence of their progeny,"

Ningul said. "If two paranormals get together, the offspring will be one or the other. Not both, and not half. When…if Fiona and I marry and have children, they will be centaurs or kelpies. They will not be half-and-half."

Fiona blushed.

"Witch and human pairings produce mixed offspring," Uncle Phil said. "It is the only pairing that does. The Witches Council is against that taking place. They believe it dilutes witch magic."

"That's absurd! I've seen Gunther do magic. There's nothing diluted about what he does," I pointed out. "I never would have known he wasn't a full witch. Heck, I'm more human than he is. There's nothing human about him. I just…I never would've known. Seriously."

"You would have if you and he tried to go visit a paranormal town," Ningul pointed out.

"What you mean?"

"He would have twinkled as brightly as a light bulb. It's an enchantment on the towns to ensure that all human-paranormals are detectable."

"That's ridiculous!"

"That's the enchantment." Ningul shrugged.

"If that's true, how did we not know this? Gunther went to a paranormal school, didn't he?"

"He went to the Imperial Academy," Uncle

Phil said. "That's for children of the Witches Council only. They don't even allow those children out on the town. It would not be hard at all to obscure his origins from all except the Council and their offspring."

"There is a reason many of us dislike witches, present company excluded," Fiona told me. "They claim the enchantment is there for the safety of the half-witch, to let people know they are more 'delicate' and easily damaged."

"That's a bundle of malarkey," Uncle Phil scoffed. "It's there to make them feel like outcasts. Hard to feel comfortable when you're putting off enough light to make a city block glow."

"But he doesn't glow here."

"The Witches Council does not command us, Charlotte."

"Not that they don't wake up every morning and devise ways to try, eh?" Fiona said.

"While this is all quite fascinating, I would like to formally request the recovery of my mate, Ringmaster," Serena said in a manner that was not precisely a request.

"Serena's right. I need to go get Mark, and I need to talk to Gunther."

In three months, I had not physically left the safety of the Magical Midway. But it was time.

I needed to grab Mark and bring him back, but I also needed to talk to Roland and Gunther Makepeace. There was no doubt in my mind that if the Magical Midway fell, the Witches Council would turn on the Makepeace Circus and Gunther next.

"We also need to get Roland Makepeace to work with us. If we're each fighting this independently, we won't achieve as much. We may even undermine each other without realizing."

"You're going to travel to Makepeace alone?" Uncle Phil looked shocked. "How do we know Roland wasn't part of the conspiracy to kidnap Mark?"

"Yes, I am, and I don't think he was. I don't know why, but I don't. He's afraid of what's going on, too." I stood up. "Look, the ringmasters have been too insular, and *every one of them* has fallen. It's just us left. If one of us can find a solution, it will work for both. Divided, I think we're both in trouble."

"It's lunch, so you only have about six hours before dusk," Uncle Phil explained while I changed behind my room divider. "Before the sun sets, get back here. The sky cannot transition from moon to sun or sun to moon with you someplace else."

And I cannot go with you, Samson said. *I must remain here to fasten your tie to the Magical Midway. We cannot interact while you are at the Makepeace Circus.*

"Be back by sundown, can't talk to Samson. Got it." I nodded, snatched up my bag, and raced into the main room. "How do I get back?"

"Just close your eyes and ask to be returned to the Magical Midway. You will be teleported to the spot you left instantaneously, like a rubber band snapping back."

Rubber band symbolism was used a lot more in magic than I would have expected.

I will ensure that when you teleport to the Makepeace Circus, you arrive at the gate. Once you have visited more, you'll be able to visualize for yourself where on the grounds you wish to appear, if they allow it. The gate is proper for your first physical visit. I nodded again.

"Is there any protocol or diplomatic greeting or something I should know about?"

You will be unwelcome no matter what you say.

"Fantastic," I muttered.

"Charlotte, just keep in mind their circus is not run the same as ours. They have their own regulations, their own customs. Their own justice."

"Am I in any danger?"

"Not *specifically*," Uncle Phil responded. "Your substantial defensive protection will travel with you, but you *cannot* influence anything with the ringmaster power there. You will have words and whatever witchcraft you can perform."

"Got it."

I threw a few more things in my bag. At the last second, I tossed a couple of bottles of water in there. With no real idea of what I was wandering into, the vulnerability I had to poison crossed my mind.

Not that I expected anyone at the Makepeace Circus wanted to kill me.

Well, at least not yet.

"Can I bring anyone with me?"

"Only one person. But if you do that, you'll not be able to return with Mark. You must go back and forth, and that could be dangerous for whoever you leave. They could work to explicitly block you."

"Can I change that?"

No, Samson replied.

Another day, another addendum to my superpower.

"Ok, I think I'm ready." I dropped my bag to the chair and checked myself in the mirror. I looked at my boots, jeans, utility belt, and work shirt. I carried a knife and a canteen besides the two bottles of water in my bag. If my head was shaved, I would have looked a little bit like Anya. I looked kind of tough, actually.

"Enough preening. Close your eyes and request to be brought to the Makepeace Circus, and remember—you *must* return by sundown." Uncle Phil handed me my bag. I blushed and took it from him.

"Oh, yeah, about that. What happens if I don't?"

"You cannot return until sunrise, and if the Magical Midway is attacked, there will be no ringmaster here to defend it."

I gulped. "Can I change *that*?"

Uncle Phil shook his head no.

I rolled my eyes, closed them, and then asked to visit the Makepeace Circus. The familiar whoosh echoed in my ears, and my skin tingled. The odor in the air changed, and I opened my eyes.

CHAPTER 9

EVERYTHING WAS GRAY.

The sky looked threatening, and I heard thunder roll in the distance. The ticket counters to my right were closed and shuttered. No humans moved within the central thoroughfare I could see.

With no lights, no visitors, and the ugly weather overhead my early impression of the Makepeace Circus without the glowing spirit energy was not a good one. I felt a sense of foreboding.

"Who you?"

A creature I had never seen before stomped toward me, grunting his query. His body was silvery with a sheen of malleable stone, and his face was grim. Razor sharp teeth jutted from his slobbering mouth while his eyes gleamed crimson.

"I am Charlotte Astley, ringmaster of the Magical Midway. I am here to speak to the Makepeaces." I was glad my words sounded calm. The creature was at least twice my height, and he was watching me like he wanted to bite me.

I prayed my uncle was correct about my defenses being sufficient here. I suspected this thing was about to test that certainty.

"They say nothing 'bout you!" The creature crouched and adjusted his weapon in front of my face. "How I know you ringmaster? You could be bad witch! Are you evil witch? Don't like bad witches."

"I am not an evil witch," I declared to him. "I'm a good witch, I promise." Granted, Gunther might want to dispute my witch performance being classed as *good*. "I only want to talk to Gunther and Roland. If you could be so kind as to let them know I am here, that would be wonderful."

The slobbering stone creature tilted his head as he contemplated my words. Behind him, I saw two new creatures just as ugly and sinister-looking as he was. Their swords were drawn, and their eyes blazed more brilliantly as they stalked closer. "She says she ringmaster. Want to talk to boss and half-breed."

I grimaced at the classification of Gunther as a half-breed.

"Yes, could one of you gentlemen please let them know I'm here?" I requested again. I leaned around the animated, slobbering statue. The first creature sprang to life and howled, drawing his blade back while I gawked at him in shock. With a grunt, he sliced toward me with it, and I froze, readied for impact.

The colossal broadsword bounced off me with a clink.

Oh, thank goodness.

"Stupid ringmaster. She real ringmaster. Stupid shield," the first creature muttered as he slumped. "You tell boss?"

"I tell boss," one of the creatures behind him said, his gigantic sword dragging on the ground as he shuffled away murmuring. "Would rather chop her up. Stupid ringmaster."

"While we're waiting, could you tell me—what are you?"

"Gargoyle. Stupid ringmaster not see gargoyle before? You not have gargoyles at you circus?"

"No." I shook my head. "Our security unit is lares guards."

"Gargoyles can beat lares guards," the first gargoyle said proudly.

"What's your name?"

"Ambom," Ambom answered, studying me with curiosity. He pointed to the gargoyle standing behind him. "That Irum." Irum stared at me wide-eyed.

"It's nice to meet you both. Like I said, I'm Charlotte," I told him and held out my hand hoping ringmaster diplomacy could help decrease the tension. Ambom looked at my extended hand with bewilderment, his flaming eyes fading to a dull orange hue. He shifted his head one way, and then another way as he considered it. Then he raised his eyes. "You shake it," I said. "Just take my hand, and pump it up and down gently once. It's a greeting. It means we intend to be friends."

"Never touch ringmaster," Ambom shook his head. "Against orders. Bad things happen. Terrible things."

"I touch half-breed once," Irum said while nodding. "Ringmaster very furious."

"What happens when your ringmaster gets mad?"

"Charlotte? *What* are you doing here?" Gunther asked as he walked toward me. His face looked pale and strained as if he hadn't relaxed in days. It was a significant transformation from the happy, casual attitude of a few days ago when he came for my magic lesson.

"Official business, really," I called and stepped toward him. "Mark Botsworth is being kept on your grounds in a barn by someone named Deo. I came here to bring him home."

"You must be mistaken."

"I'm afraid not."

"Are you sure? I have heard nothing about this." Gunther asked, shocked. I sensed the confusion was genuine, and nodded that I was sure.

"I am. I also know you guys got a visit from the Witches Council. I thought this might be something we need to talk about."

I skipped mentioning I knew Gunther was half-human. I didn't know enough about the Makepeace Circus, Roland, or Gunther's relationship with his father to poke at that just yet. It was clear from what I saw last night there was tension around Gunther's origins. I didn't know enough about anything to wade into that confusion, and my immediate worry was Mark. For the moment, anyway.

"Do you know what barn Mark's supposed to

be in?" Gunther said as he gestured for me to follow him. "I can't believe any of our people would be involved in that, but Deo...well, he's kind of arrogant. I hope you're wrong."

"I'm not. I wish I was, though."

As we walked through the main thoroughfare, I felt eyes peering out from behind gleaming festival stands. The Makepeace Circus was as spotless, bright, and new in reality as it looked through the blue rose haze. Nothing about it seemed used or old. Compared to the Magical Midway, Makepeace appeared wholly contemporary, and we appeared totally old-fashioned. Even the path we walked on was graded and neatly graveled.

"That one!" I told him, pointing at a large gray barn. "I'm almost positive it's that one."

Gunther and I raced to the outbuilding and tugged on the door, but we were both unable to open it. "It's...locked somehow. But there's no lock on these doors. I mean, they shouldn't even be *able* to lock. It's just feed storage." Gunther rattled the massive doors further, tugging harder, but they would not open.

Stepping backward, Gunther narrowed his eyes and flashed his palms toward the door. With a shower of pink fire, the door blew open with a crash. I jumped.

"Hello?" Mark called from within. Running into the barn, I found him where I had left him the night before. "Nice to see you again, Charlotte!" Mark smiled. "I was guessing you had gotten held up. Or forgot about me."

"Not a chance, Botsworth," I told him as Gunther cast spells to remove Mark's irons. "Can you stand?"

"I think so," he said and supported himself against the wall unsteadily.

"Wait here," I told Gunther. "I need to get him back to our circus."

"You can't leave, my Dad will want to find out how this happened! We need to talk to him. He'll want to talk to Mark, I'm sure."

"I get it. But no."

"Charlotte—"

"No offense, Gunther, but *I* can't be hurt here. *He* can be. I'm not leaving him here another second for any reason when we do not understand how he's here or why he was taken."

I could see Gunther wanted to argue with me, but he finally nodded and stepped back. "Come right back. I'll be right here."

It was remarkably simple to just pop back to the Magical Midway with another person in tow. Though my mind was distracted with everything I'd learned in the last day, I had a job to do, and it felt like I was getting better at it.

"Mark!" Serena sobbed as we emerged in my yurt. The calm and elegant lion shifter raced across the room to seize her missing partner. My uncle, Samson, Fiona, and Ningul jumped up from their seats and followed her. "Oh my, oh my Mark!" The couple wrapped their arms around one another.

"I'm okay, I'm here. Serena, it will be okay."

"It will not be okay!" Serena wailed, her face hidden in his chest. "I cannot lose you. I don't care what regulations the Witches Council claims we have broken. I will kill them before I allow them to take you." Mark, still unsteady on his feet, folded her tighter in his arms and caressed her head while she sobbed. Mark raised his tormented eyes to meet mine but spoke nothing.

"I need to get back there," I told the group. "We still don't know why he was taken."

"Did you find out whether the Makepeaces knew about Mark?" Fiona said. "Surely, they

knew Mark was at their circus. I mean, how
could they not?"

"I don't know that's the case," I disagreed.
"When I first showed up last night, Roland was
speaking to their people. I sensed nothing from
him, or from Gunther, that showed they knew
what was going on. I didn't sense they took part
in taking Mark."

"How do you *not* know what is going on in
your own circus as a ringmaster?"

"We have less all-knowing superpowers than
you think we do, Fiona. I mean, I didn't know
about Dergal, and Uncle Phil over here knew so
little that he gulped down his own death.
Anyway, Gunther seemed astounded when we
located him, and he helped get Mark
unshackled."

"It's true," Mark said.

"Yeah, well, that's Gunther. That's not Roland."
Ningul rubbed Fiona's back to pacify my
indignant friend. I had to give him points for
trying, but once you wound Fiona up she pretty
much just went. "That Roland is the most—"

"He's a ringmaster. And he has as much to fear
from the Witches Council as we do."

"I hardly believe *that* to be true."

"Remember, Gunther is half-human. If he

cares about his son's life at all, he does," I told Ningul.

The room fell silent.

"I wonder how many over at their circus know about him?" Uncle Phil asked me.

"It seems like it may be an open secret over at the Makepeace Circus. Roland seemed defensive about it. What do you know about Gunther's mother, Uncle Phil?"

The Witches Council killed her, Samson told me. The all-knowing cat told me what he knew about my friend's family, and the deal Roland Makepeace struck with the Witches Council to keep his son, my friend, alive.

Gunther sat in the barn waiting just where he said he would be.

Nothing about Gunther screamed the tragedy he had been through. Did he know what his father had done to save his life? What he had given up to ensure his son would have a future? I didn't know. For the moment, though, I needed to focus on Mark's kidnapping and the showdown with the Council.

"Is there any possibility your father has a hand

in Mark being kidnapped? Would he have helped the Witches Council?" I asked.

Gunther paused for a moment and then nodded slowly.

"My father is not like your Uncle Phil. He's not like you." Gunther pointed toward a bale of hay and gestured for me to go sit down. "I love my father. I do. But…I'm not proud of a lot of the things he does, though. Or the way he treats the people that live here."

"What do you mean?" I sat down and tucked my feet up beneath me. Gunther sat a small distance away.

"This is a fiefdom to him. I mean, both of the circuses are fiefdoms, really," he smiled, reminding me of my omnipotence. "But my father *treats* it like one. He looks at himself like a feudal lord and all the people that live here like peasants obligated to him. Dad is the worst combination of witchcraft elitism and ringmaster control. It's crazy."

"I see." My mind flashed on moments with the people of the Magical Midway that concerned me. Ningul's panic I would slaughter all of the centaurs when Dergal tried to poison me. Avalon's fear I would withdraw protection from the weredeers. Perhaps their apprehensive attitude toward me came from memory, not paranoia. "Is he just rude, or does he run roughshod over these people?"

"Dad has the power of death and banishment over everyone at the Makepeace Circus. He uses it. Sometimes unfairly, sometimes when a lesser punishment would have gotten the point across. It's happened two or three times that I remember. But his willingness to use it impacts people."

"Why do you think he's so strict?" I told him.

"A few of the older residents told me he wasn't always this way. A gorgon killed my mother, and it devastated him. My father decided that paranormals needed a 'strong hand' to control them after that, and so he took one. He blamed himself for her death, maybe. I don't think he ever got over it."

Gunther didn't seem to know that the Witches Council may have had a hand in the death of his mother. I contemplated telling him what I had just discovered, but remained silent. I didn't understand what it all meant yet. Instead, I resolved to address the half-human elephant in the room.

"Your mother was human?" Gunther's eyes grew wide with shock.

"How did you know?"

"I heard what happened last night at the meeting," I told him without getting into the specifics of how I heard it.

Gunther shifted in his chair and rubbed his eyes. He nodded again.

"Yes, I'm half-human." Gunther got up and looked down at me. "Go ahead. Get it out."

"Get *what* out?" I asked, confused.

"Whatever snide remark you're going to say. I'm used to it. I know full-blooded witches despise people like me. Hell, I'm not even supposed to exist, so I should be grateful you all allow me to breathe, right?"

I should have expected it after what Samson told me, but I didn't.

It was a shock. Painful. For three months, we had talked of our lives, laughed over jokes, and ducked flying items together. Did Gunther believe that I thought less of him because of who his mother was?

"Gunther...I'm not like all those full-blooded witches. Come on. I don't care who your Mom was. I don't think any differently of you now than I did two days ago. Heck, you *should* be more like them. You went to the Witches Academy. I'm curious, though—*how* did you go to the Witches Academy? Didn't you glow?"

I felt like a jerk manipulating his story from him as if I didn't already know.

"Yep," he blew his breath out slowly. "Like a star atop a Christmas tree."

I pictured a young Gunther attending school with young, immature versions of Mina, Mabel, and Mercy. If young witches were anything like their adult judgmental counterparts, school must've been absolutely miserable for Gunther. "Gunther, I'm so sorry…"

"You didn't push me into a magic chest every day," he smiled.

"Still. You were a child. That must have been really hard for you."

"My mother hated it, and fought it," Gunther sighed, staring off into the distance. "But she died. My father decided after her death it would toughen me up, being subjected to the derision of the witch community. Schooling with the elite of the elites. Not *everyone* was horrible. The mean students always seemed to take the lead, though. No one wanted to be next, so no one stuck up for me. I learned to grin and bear it."

"It seems to be like that everywhere," I admitted. "I was kind of an outcast in school, too, but I didn't glow to advertise it to everybody. It's like *The Scarlet Letter* for kids."

"What's *The Scarlet Letter*?"

"Never mind. It's not important." My own father was determined that my upbringing take place far from the paranormal community, and my mother never fought him particularly hard on the idea. There weren't all that many witches left in the world—a few hundred at best, and so I never felt like I missed out on much.

The more I found out about my fellow witches, the more I was grateful for my father's decisions. I'd rather have a rough start as ringmaster than grow up with the elitist prejudices that the witch community seemed to demand.

"Charlotte?" I shook off my thoughts and focused back on Gunther. "You looked a million miles away there for a second."

"I was just thinking. I just wonder how any group winds up so…corrupted, I guess. It just makes me sad that the paranormal world is like this. The more I find out about it, the more I'm just…it's just sad, that's all."

"Well, not the *whole* paranormal world. The Magical Midway isn't like this. And we have our moments here, too, you know. It's not all bad. So, we're still here. We're not gone yet."

"Not yet," I agreed, then sighed. "If the

Witches Council has its way, we will be. Let's go talk to your Dad."

"You don't want to talk to Deo first?"

"This isn't my circus," I told him. "Your Dad's the ringmaster here. I think I should talk to him first before I go poking around his fiefdom."

CHAPTER 10

ROLAND MAKEPEACE'S COTTAGE WOULD NOT HAVE looked out of place at an upscale ski lodge. The timber's rich brown color shone as if it had been waxed, and the deck wrapped around the width of the massive structure. Homey rocking chairs were strewn around next to side tables. The coziness of the decor seemed at odds with Roland's stormy temperament.

"My Mom," Gunther said upon seeing my confusion. "Dad changed nothing she did."

Gunther knocked on the door and called out to his father. He then opened the door without waiting for a response. "Dad, Charlotte Astley is here to talk to you. We're coming in."

"Is this situation not tense enough without

your little girlfriend coming to muddle it up even more?" Roland's angry voice thundered from somewhere above. I looked up to see the haggard man descending the stairs. His boots stomped loudly as he clomped down to the living room.

"Mr. Makepeace, it's good to see you again," I greeted him as he stepped into the expansive living area. "You have a lovely home."

"It's a mausoleum," he snapped and hiccuped. I noticed that he was unstable on his feet, eyes glassy. "A monument I haunt every single day, girl. I'd pass on your compliments to my wife," he sneered as he slammed down on a couch. "But she's *dead*." He pulled out a flask and guzzled from it.

Gunther remained silent.

"You seem a little unsteady on your feet, Mr. Makepeace. Are you drinking? I only ask because when I drink, I can't even get tipsy," I told him, sitting down beside him. I smiled at the troubled man as I tried to engage him in friendly conversation. "How do you manage that? The drinking, I mean?"

"You Astleys, you always had a stick up your tail about playing it safe. We Makepeaces had no such worry." Roland hiccuped again and took another guzzle. "We've been drinking for generations, and nothing bad has ever taken place."

Gunther dropped his eyes to a picture next to Roland of a beautiful blond woman holding a cheerful three-year-old, and his eyes shined with unshed tears.

"Mr. Makepeace, I wanted to talk to you about some of the things that have been going on. Well, two things, really. I rescued Mark Botsworth from your feed barn. A member of your community, Deo, kidnapped him. I'd like your permission to talk to Deo to see if I can determine why he was taken."

"Talk to him," Roland waved at me without commenting on Mark's kidnapping. "Take him. What do I care? We're all doomed, anyway." Gunther's father hiccuped again and swallowed more from the flask. "Your elevation has brought the Witches Council down upon us all!"

"Dad, come on." Gunther moved to sit on the other side of his father. "It's not Charlotte's fault."

"Says the halfling," Roland mumbled. The big man removed his hat and threw it at Gunther. "Go on, take it. See if it fits, boy. I failed my Gerda, no doubt I will fail you, my son." Roland's head fell back on the couch, and he let out a loud snore. Even in his boozy sleep, I could feel the intense emotional pain and frustration swimming through his drunken dreams.

"I'm sorry," Gunther said. We sat and watched his unconscious father between us.

"Don't apologize. I'm just…I'm just surprised, that's all. Between your father's condescending attempt at buying my circus and his speech last night, I wouldn't have pictured…well, this," I motioned to his inebriated father. "Your father is in an extraord*inary* amount of pain. It's coming off him in waves."

Gunther sighed. "I know. I mean, I can't sense it like you can. But I have eyes. My father's not a happy man."

"That may be the understatement of the year," I told him and then bit my lip. "Look, I'm sorry. I didn't mean to be flippant about it. Sometimes this all strikes me as so ridiculously dramatic it all *seems* like a joke or a comedy of errors I can't escape from. But it's not. This isn't a joke, and I'm sorry. This can't be easy for you."

"When he's drunk, he says he loves me," Gunther said. "When he's sober, he's angry and dismissive of me. I don't…my memories of him as a child were not of this man. My parents were happy. He was kind once."

"How old were you when your mother passed away?"

"Nine years old. We went for a walk to pick wildflowers for my father. My mother would do little things like that." He smiled and leaned back. "My father could manifest anything she wanted, anything at all. But she loved to do it the old-fashioned way."

"The human way."

"Maybe." Gunther fell silent, and I waited for him to finish the story or add to it, but he didn't.

"He assured everyone that the Witches Council would not come after you. Do you think that was a lie? Has he said you're threatened in any way?"

"No, but I don't know that he would tell me if I was." Gunther got up and leaned over his father, extracting the flask from his hand. He pointed to a rainbow-colored afghan sitting next to me, and I handed it to him so he could wrap his father in it. I could see, clearly, the love that Gunther had for his turbulent father even though he felt hurt by him. Family relationships are so complicated.

Ringmaster families may be the most complex of all.

∼

After we dimmed the lights and tucked Roland in, we left the log cabin to find Deo.

"Why didn't you accuse my father of being involved in the kidnapping?" Gunther asked. "I mean, I wouldn't blame you if you thought he was doing it to move against you. Especially considering how rude he was to you when you first met."

"Rudeness and kidnapping aren't necessarily related." As we walked through the circus grounds, eyes peeked out at us from every direction. "I knew he was telling the truth to your folks last night. Well, wait—I knew he was telling the truth about feeling like it had nothing to do with you. I sensed nothing from him to show I should suspect him."

"That's a handy talent to have, I guess."

"Especially for a lawgiver."

Gunther stopped mid-stride and turned to face me. "Wait a second. *You've* been made a *lawgiver?*"

"Yeah, my uncle thought it would help me to be more social with the folks at the Magical Midway. I have been spending a lot of time with close friends and…well, and you." Gunther smiled warmly at me in response, and my heart skipped a beat.

Must be heartburn. Yeah, that's definitely it. Heartburn because of all the stress I was under. Kidnappings, Witches Councils, greedy naiads and crazy lion shifters. It was heartburn and anxiety, and not the way the wind blew through his golden hair or the way he—

Heartburn. The end.

We were staring at each other and not talking. For too long. I stepped back and coughed.

"You need some water?" I shook my head no. "Well, good luck. Being a lawgiver is a pretty intense gig. Mabel's going to have apoplexy."

"Oh, yeah? Why?" I asked, scanning for a lion shifter while we walked.

"Reforming society is a big responsibility," Gunther said. "Writing laws, enacting them, enforcing them."

"Isn't that what I do for the Magical Midway, anyway? Ringmaster omnipotence and all that stuff? I think he just wanted to come up with something that I could make my own, you know?" Gunther nodded. "It doesn't sound all that much different than what I was told ringmasters do, anyway."

"Oh, it's *quite* a bit different," Gunther laughed. I looked at him and raised my eyebrow. "It gets you a vote on the Witches Council."

"It gets me *a what now?*" I shouted at him and grabbed his arm. Heads popped out like a shot from behind curtains and inside of windows. Gunther looked around and waved at the faces painted with concern, and they slowly disappeared back into the darkness. Turning back he smiled again.

"Your uncle didn't tell you this?"

"No!"

"That's why there are no lawgivers anymore," Gunther said. "The Witches Council slowly voted them obsolete. Only the circuses still have their seats, if they choose to take them, because of the bloodline stuff."

"Okay, wait a minute, the circuses all could have appointed lawgivers to sit on the Witches Council? And they didn't? There were way more of them than there were of those witches that *aren't* from circuses. Why would they not go and correct some of this garbage that goes on in the witch world?"

"They didn't care, I guess?" Gunther shrugged. "I suspect the ringmasters were always suspicious of other ringmasters. Friendly but distant was the closest anyone ever got. The relationship you and I have..." He paused.

"It's not normal? Common?"

"Everyone protected their own circus, their own people. The ringmasters would have needed to join together to plan some kind of coup, and there's nothing in our history to suggest they were ever friendly enough to do that. The Council divided and conquered."

"So over hundreds of years, that power was just ignored? Never used?"

"Yep."

"Now you and I are meandering through the backyard trying to uncover plots to take us out because they just didn't *bother* to vote?" Maybe it was my human upbringing or my public human schooling, but these influential people trading a vote in how the world evolves for small pond power just incensed me.

"Well, when you put it like *that*, it sounds bad. But yeah, pretty much."

As we walked behind an enormous, shining roller coaster, Delilah ran up to Gunther and patted his shoe. "Hey, there, little one," Gunther cooed as he leaned over to pluck the tiny cat off the ground. "Slow down there, speedy, and tell me again?" His face steadied as he stared Delilah in the eye and they interacted with each other.

There is nothing as hot as a handsome guy with a kitten.

Heartburn, darn it.

"Delilah says that Deo is in the pub."

"You have a pub?"

"Don't you?"

"No."

"Well, where do you guys go to just hang out together when there's a big group?"

"We had that big party under the big top once."

"You should get a pub," Gunther said as he deposited the kitten on his shoulder. "It's important for folks to have someplace casual to go hang out as a group. Otherwise, everyone stays with their own group in their living areas and no one mixes. Or they stay in their house, and no one ever sees them."

"Like me, you mean. You're talking about me."

"I would never say such things about a lawgiver."

I could swear that kitten laughed.

～

Gunther wasn't kidding. It was a full-on fancy pub. In the middle of a circus. Huh.

We sat down at one of ten tables arranged around the wooden structure. The distinctions between the Makepeace Circus and the Magical Midway were sharper here. Almost all at the Magical Midway looked impermanent on the surface by design, an old-fashioned tent circus with smaller trailer structures. That they never moved wasn't the issue. They needed to look like they could.

The Makepeaces had no such apprehensions about human curiosity judging by their design. While most of the structures were log cottages and could, theoretically, be taken down and moved, it would require far more trucks than their circus had. The rides were extensive and more permanent-looking than our own.

"Don't you worry that patrons will question that all this is here?" I asked Gunther after he ordered two fizzies for us from a sultry waitress. I didn't know what a fizzy was, but I wasn't planning on drinking it, anyway. Poison. Didn't want to be poisoned on top of all the other issues I was dealing with.

"There's an obfuscation spell permanently on the grounds. Has been for a few generations. No one really questions, not even local law enforcement."

"That's pretty smart." I swiveled my head

looking for Deo. "So what do you know about Deo?"

"Not much," Gunther replied as the waitress placed two pink and blue drinks in front of us. He nodded and smiled, and she bowed slightly in return. "He's been here five or six years, maybe? We only have five lion shifters, and they keep to themselves. Try the fizzy, you'll like it."

I shook my head. "I'm pretty careful with what I eat or drink these days." I checked the time on my watch and saw it was late afternoon. "Do you see Deo? I will have to get out of here soon."

Gunther scanned the crowded room. "There," he pointed to the back corner behind the bar. "He's in the back corner booth over there."

I stretched to look over folks sitting and having a good time, and saw Deo tucked into the booth. He sat in the far back corner next to another lion shifter, and it looked like that other lion shifter was letting him have it.

"So, how do we do this? I don't have any powers, and you're not a ringmaster. Can your magic hold him?"

"What do you mean you don't have any powers?" Gunther asked, perplexed. "You're a lawgiver. If he's guilty, you can do almost anything to him."

"Even here at your circus?"

"Anywhere. Paranormal towns, other circuses."

"How did I suddenly get all this power? My uncle and I just had a chat. There has to be more involved than that."

"Did you get the lawgiver ring?" I held up my hand to show Gunther the small, thin, plain ring that now encircled my finger. "The power is yours. You can't give it back or lay it down now."

"What do you mean?" I asked, confused. I grabbed the ring and tugged, but it didn't move so much as a millimeter. "Oh, you must be kidding me. It won't come off!"

"You don't get a whole lot of knowledge from your uncle before you agree to do things, do you?" Gunther asked.

"They're supposed to be training me! I assume they'd tell me anything I needed to know beforehand!"

"Charlotte, you have to qualify some of this stuff a little better." Gunther's face grew thoughtful, and he leaned in. "I have no doubt they believed this role to be a good one for you, and I agree with them. I think it's cool. If I could do it, I would."

"Why can't you?"

"I'm half-human. The ring just falls off my finger. My father tried. He thought making me lawgiver would protect me from the Witches Council if they ever made a move against me." Gunther shrugged. "It didn't work."

Heartburn again. We sat across the table, looking into one another's eyes. I reminded myself of what my family had warned me about. Gunther was to be the ringmaster here, and I was already the ringmaster of the Magical Midway. We both had obligations and magical constraints that ensured any relationship between us could never work.

Well, okay, it would be hard. Less than twelve-hour dates during the day or during the night. We couldn't live together. But people make long distance relationships work all the time, didn't they?

Stop it, Charlotte.

"Are you all right? I'm sorry if I…never mind. Are you ready to talk to him?"

"How do I use the power of the ring?"

"I know 'freeze' works if you come upon the guilty party, so that should restrain him if Mark is correct about who kidnapped him."

"Just 'freeze'? Like a cop drawing a gun on a suspect?"

"Where do you think they got it from?"

Good point.

We made our way over to the booth. Deo spotted us halfway across the darkened room. He jumped up to get away and scrambled over the lion shifter that had been lecturing him. I took a deep breath and shouted.

"Freeze, Deo!"

Well, that worked better than I expected. The lion shifter not only froze in a particularly inelegant position (with one leg hanging in the air and his entire body at a ridiculous angle over the table), but the rest of the revelers also fell silent and stared at me with apprehension.

I ignored everyone else and slid into the booth. Gunther slipped into the other side, penning the two lion shifters in the corner. "Sit down," I told the contorted lion shifter, and he did, facing me. Deo looked like Leo, he of the expensive French conditioner. So much so I suspected they were related, if not twins.

"Do you know who I am?"

"A *witch*," Deo hissed.

"I'm Charlotte Astley of the Magical Midway.

You kidnapped one of my people, Mark Botsworth," I told him as his eyes widened. "I want to know why."

"I don't have to answer your questions," Deo said. "You are in league with the enemy, half-breed. Your father would be sickened by your betrayal."

"Charlotte asked his permission before coming to question you," Gunther told him. "So, get off your high unicorn, Deo. Answer her questions. She's a lawgiver so she can make you comply. I don't think you want her to do that."

"A dimwitted witch that lived in the human world—a ringmaster, and now a lawgiver? It's as bad as the half-human supposed heir we are stuck with here," Deo seethed as his eyes narrowed. Gunther stared back unflinching, his face calm. Deo's attack bounced off him as if it didn't bother him at all.

"Be that as it may, lion shifter, you kidnapped one of the residents of her circus. Neither she or my father will be very pleased with you if you continue this bravado. Talk. Now."

Wow, that formal ringmaster speech talent Gunther has is super hot.

I must be catching a cold. Besides the heartburn, I'm getting the shivers. Is it cold in here? It must be cold in here. Or maybe I'm getting sick.

"I did it for the Makepeace Circus. I was just going to keep him until the end of the week and then shove him back on the grounds when the seven days were up. I didn't hurt him."

"What would that accomplish?" I asked.

"It would ensure that you had a human on your grounds when the Witches Council came to make you pay. It would ensure you had no time to find a way out of your *just* punishment."

"Make me pay for what? Punishment for what?"

Deo clamped his mouth shut and glared at me. I waited, but the lion shifter would say no more. I looked at Gunther, and then back to Deo. Then I had an idea.

"Well, at least Leo is dead, and we won't have to worry about him," I told Gunther offhand and scooted out of the booth. My little white lie caused a contained explosion from the mostly frozen lion shifter.

"You stupid witch! I will ensure that you are eaten by the fiercest of lions in retribution for the death of my brother! He only became involved in this plot to protect Serena and guard his pride! He never would have worked with the

Witches Council if you ringmasters guarded the old laws!"

"Hush, now," I told Deo, and his mouth snapped shut. I could get used to this lawgiver thing. So far, it seemed to work just like the ringmaster power. This could be a pretty convenient power to have.

As I sat back down, I grabbed a napkin and wiped Deo's spittle from my arm. The lion shifter sitting next to Deo had remained silent for the entire exchange, but now his shoulders slumped, and he buried his head in his hands.

"And what's your feeling about all this?" The second shifter raised his head and looked at me with a raised eyebrow. "Yes, you. You don't look too thrilled with your compadre over there."

"Leo and Deo are angry lions, ma'am. Their mother thought they would be better off at the circus with my wife and me," he responded. "She thought they'd get discipline, a work ethic. The boys are a little bit on the entitled side, but this is far beyond what any of us thought they would do."

"Charlotte, this is Bubba," Gunther said.

"Bubba McAfee, Ms. Charlotte," the man said as he stuck out his hand. The older lion shifter had a distinct southern drawl and dressed like he had just finished at a garage for the day. "Pleased to make your acquaintance. My apologies for the trouble my nephews have caused you."

"Bubba is the pride leader at the Makepeace Circus, Charlotte. His family has been with us for two generations."

"But not Deo? And Leo and Deo are brothers?"

"Twins, ma'am," Bubba nodded. "My sister, Lula Bell, asked me to take her boys when they were a little bit more than she could handle. Leo used to be here a few years ago until he met that naiad and ran away to your circus."

"Naiad?"

"Alexa Atwater," Bubba said and sighed. "That girl had Leo so twisted up the boy thought up was down and down was up."

Deo jerked and vibrated within his invisible magical encasement, his eyes waggling as if he wanted to protest. The enchantment around him was tight enough that not even a moan escaped from him, but he stared daggers at his uncle.

"Leo left the Makepeace Circus to chase that girl from town to town. She left *him* for bigger and better things, so I heard. I tried to get him to come back, but then the pride leader at Magical Midway died and he saw his chance to lead. A chance he never could have earned on his own."

I leaned back and crossed my arms. "Since he was the only male, when he showed up he got to be in charge? Even though he was new and young, and clearly much more of a jerk than the women?"

"Now, young lady, I didn't make the rules. I just live in a world with them. But yep," Bubba nodded. "I reckon that's pretty much how it happened. With no one to challenge Leo, he was in charge."

"I swear, the paranormal world is like stepping back in time," I muttered to myself. "Did Leo really help Deo kidnap Mark? It seems kind of obvious considering they're brothers and what Deo just said, but I'd like to be sure exactly what role he played. He's not dead—that was a little bit of trickery on my part."

"We were talking about it when y'all walked in," Bubba nodded. "I was giving the boy what for when y'all moseyed on over here. From what I understand, Leo pushed Mark off the circus grounds, and Deo snatched him up and held him for his brother."

"Leo was pretty unhappy that one of the lionesses, Serena, was dating Mark. I guess that could be part of the reason he made sure Mark would be on the grounds when the Witches Council came to pass their judgment. That doesn't just get rid of Mark, though."

"What do you mean?" Gunther asked.

"There are two things that Mina demanded of us. One is that we hand over Mark and Fortuna, and she made it *clear* they would be killed once we did. The second is that we take the barrier down and subject ourselves to their rules. Basically, we have to unblock any protection that enables us to escape their punishment, enforcement, or judgment." Gunther considered what I said.

"You think the Witches Council engineered this kidnapping? Like some kind of plot on top of their demand? But why? What do they get out of it?"

"I doubt Deo here had any knowledge of that," Bubba said. "Honestly, ma'am, the boy is not that bright."

"Neither is Leo, I'm sure. He struck me as arrogant, but not particularly brilliant," I agreed. "Alexa Atwater, though, is another story. She struck me as smart and conniving."

"She is that, ma'am," Bubba nodded.

"I still don't see what she gets out of it, though.

Speak," I told Deo. He gasped and gulped air as his mouth fell open.

"I'm not telling you anything," Deo snapped. "I'm not gonna sit here and listen to you call my brother and me stupid. He's a pride leader. We don't have to take this from you. You'll be replaced soon, anyway. You, and this half-breed. Alexa promised—"

If you get them angry enough, they can't help running their mouths.

I looked at my watch and jumped. "I can't stay here anymore. I have to get back."

"What do you want us to do with him, lawgiver?" Gunther smiled and winked at me.

"When your father...um, wakes up from his nap?" I said. "Let him know what's gone on. Deo is yours, so I'll leave it to your father to decide what to do with them. Until then, Deo?" I leaned down and stared into Deo's eyes. "You may not leave the Makepeace Circus grounds. You may not communicate with your brother. In fact, you may not speak to anyone until you tell Gunther and Roland the full story of what you have done and why."

Deo opened his mouth to shout at me, but no sound came out.

"I like this lawgiver thing," I smiled. "Gunther,

I'll be back tomorrow, as soon as I sort out this kidnapping thing. Your Dad and I still have to discuss how we're going to deal with the Witches Council. Make sure, if you can, that he's awake?"

"Will do, Charlotte. And be careful."

"She's a ringmaster and a lawgiver. What could hurt her?" Bubba asked.

As I asked to be rubber-banded back to the Magical Midway, I knew something could, and I would discover what that is at some point, if history was any indication.

CHAPTER 11

You cut it close. We were getting concerned, Samson beamed into my brain the moment I materialized. *Did you find out anything helpful?*

Leo helped push Mark off the grounds, and then a lion shifter from Makepeace held him. They would bring Mark back on the day the Council was due to arrive back here. Alexa may have had something to do with it, I told him as I walked toward my yurt. The sun was nearly below the horizon, and the sky was bathed in a deep orange. Samson was right, I came back with only minutes to spare. *I think I want to talk to Leo first. Oh, and by the way...*

Yes?

A seat on the Witches Council? Really?

Your young man has a big mouth, Samson grumbled.

But is what his big mouth said correct?

Let's deal with one thing at a time, shall we?

I nodded at a passing goblin that waved and sighed. I was getting used to the fact that information was not eagerly given by my loyal familiar, but I had a creeping suspicion there was more to it than his attitude. Samson knew things I didn't and had resolved that for some reason, I had to earn information even if he had it. Thinking back on it, I never asked him why.

Everyone's paranormal in this world. I thought they always talked like a cheap fortune teller on a boardwalk just because they could. It was a cultural thing. As these plots and plans unfolded all around me, it seemed like it was time to ask why. Something deeper, something more profound could be going on. Something Samson was keeping from me for a reason.

Or, you know, everyone in this world was just a certifiable drama queen who enjoyed performing in their own version of "As the Fun House Barrel Turns."

It could be that, too.

As I entered my yurt, Alexa Atwater stood up from my couch and confronted me.

"Want a drink, oh, powerful ringmaster? I made this one for you." Alexa held up a cup of murky water and thrust it in my direction. As I stared at the container, the water rose from within and snaked toward me across the room, and I felt waves of triumph coming off of the naiad.

"Freeze!" I screeched, and Alexa froze with her cup extended.

The water, however, did not.

Well, fuzzbuckets, this is a problem. I sent the images as hard as I could to Samson and I ran to the other side of the room. Like a missile headed toward a laser-painted target, the snake line of water turned and slithered steadily toward me in a dogged march. "Retreat!" I yelled, gawking at the water.

Samson? I thought anxiously as the water continued its slow creep.

Get out of there, Samson replied. *Don't get pinned down in that corner, and whatever you do, don't let that water reach your nose.*

Ugh. What a way to die. Getting water shoved up my nose.

I hate getting water up my nose.

Dancing around the yurt, I confused the water's beeline for my nostrils by heading all the way into a back corner away from it. As I waited, observing it drift toward the back of the yurt, I made my move when it was only a foot from my face. Diving behind a chair to my right to impede its attack, I scurried toward the entryway and out the door.

Fire! Go toward the fire pit!

Without waiting to see if it followed me, I took off running across the path to the fire pit. "Everyone move out of the way!" I shouted at the people roaming around. "Don't let the water touch you! Stay away from it."

Like something out of a horror movie, the line of water peeked out of my yurt. After moving right, left as if it was hunting for me, the liquid slithered again in midair toward my nostrils. It seemed unable to curve itself, expanding out of my yurt in a straight line. I looked around for anything I could use to contain it.

"Charlotte, what's going on?" Uncle Phil asked as he ran up.

"Alexa tried to give me that water," I told my uncle while glaring at the three-foot cloudy liquid line. "I don't think she was concerned for my hydration levels."

"Just tell it to disappear!"

"I tried!"

Evaporate it in the fire! Samson ran up too. *Naiads use ordinary water as a base. Just get it in the fire, it should dissipate.*

I focused and made the fire bigger, reassured when my ringmaster power could still do *that*. As the snake water made its way toward me, it hit the flames I hid behind and hissed. Then it pulled back and paused.

"Oh dear unicorns, can that thing actually *think*?" I cried out. "Are you kidding me?" The intensity of the fire had only sheered about six inches off of the weaponized water.

It has to go straight, and it can't go any faster than this. Just stay alert, Samson said. *Phillip, find an Atwater sister. Any of them other than Alexa.*

"Got it," Uncle Phil said, and he thundered toward the boat ride. As I listened to his feet clomp away, I stared at the water through the flames as it stared at me. I could see gawking crowds gathering in my peripheral vision. Great. The people I am supposed to protect are watching me get cornered by a stick of determined water.

Better that than watching you get killed by one. Stay focused, Samson said.

Oh, believe me, cat, I'm super focused.

"What the heck are you doing, Charlotte?" Anya wandered through the crowd with Fortuna.

"The water! It's attacking her!" A voice called from the crowd.

"You naiads and your murderous water attacks!"

"It's always you water nymphs causing all the trouble!"

"Hey!" Anya roared. She whirled on the crowd and lifted her fists. "Back the heck off before I drown every one of you!" With a flick of her wrist, the water snake fell to the ground and splashed to its demise. I breathed a sigh of relief and leaned against the fire pit with a clang. I don't think I'll ever get used to sounding like the Tin Man.

Anya's rescue of me had done nothing to calm the crowd's resentment.

"We know it's you nymphs that called the Witches Council!"

"You're always creating trouble!"

"Why can't you go back to some river where you belong!"

"Enough!" I shouted, and the crowd silenced instantly. I didn't know whether it was out of respect or some ringmaster power, but either way, I was grateful. "With everything going on right now, the last thing we need to do is turn on one another. The Witches Council wants to see us torn apart. Let's not help them by doing it for them."

The crowd murmured to one another, some grudgingly agreeing and some complaining under their breath about the troublesome water women. No one was screaming anymore, though, so I'd take it. I had other things to deal with.

"Go on about your business, folks. When you go gossip about what you saw—and you will gossip about what you saw because that's what you do—make sure to let people know Anya saved me. Because that's the *only* thing you witnessed here, and the *only* tale you have to tell."

The crowd nodded, and slowly drifted away.

"I'm sorry about that," I told Anya and reached out for her. She glowered and shook me off.

"I'm used to it. Why were you being attacked by water?"

"Alexa." Anya closed her eyes tightly and tensed as if I slapped her.

"Please allow me to formally apologize for my idiot of a sister."

"Tell you what, I'll accept your apology if you come with me to talk to your sister. I'm sure there's more water somewhere in my yurt."

Anya glanced at my yurt as if she would rather do anything but what I asked her to do, but after a moment, she nodded.

As Anya, Fortuna, and I went into my yurt, Alexa's eyeballs scanned each face.

"To make a long story short," I said, "Deo claimed Leo helped push Mark off the grounds. His pride leader, Bubba, had a strong impression the two brothers worked at the direction of your sister, Alexa. What I can't figure out is why."

"Why what?" Fortuna asked.

"Why it would matter whether or not Mark was here. What did Mark's kidnapping gain them? I mean, they don't know him. He has no history in the paranormal world."

"Let me go get him," Fortuna said. "Maybe he knows why they would grab him and not me. Or maybe they wanted to grab me too, and I didn't give them an opportunity."

Alexa, still frozen with an empty glass outstretched, rolled her eyes.

"Yeah, go get Mark. We'll be here."

Fortuna hurried out of the yurt, leaving Anya and me alone with Alexa.

"Do you want me to unfreeze her?" I asked the pacing Anya. My tough friend looked as troubled as I had ever seen her. She stared at her sister, her eyes shining glassy. In silence, she walked back and forth nervously without responding.

You know, I thought living at a circus was supposed to be fun. Rides and shows and amusement and cotton candy. This whole gig was smacking of a grim irony I didn't find entertaining.

"Anya! I can't find out anything from your pacing and your sister's angry eyeballs. I will unfreeze her unless you think there's a reason I shouldn't. A reason like you're too preoccupied to keep me from getting drowned by the water in the toilet."

"You can't drown," she snarled.

"When I first got here, many people told me I was untouchable, and that keeps turning out *not* to be the case. Are you focused enough for me to risk my life, or should I leave her suspended and just listen to the clock tick down? I mean, we can hope at the last moment I can pull a plan out of the air, but I would prefer to be more prepared than that."

"All right, all right! I've got it!" Anya turned and glared at me. "You know, the longer you're here, the more annoying you get. Unfreeze her." Anya turned back to her sister. "I can deal with anything baby sister throws at you."

I stared at the naiad and spoke the words to unfreeze her. My body shuddered with tension as I prepared for another attack, but she made no move to do so. Crossing her arms, she plopped back down on the couch and placed the glass on the coffee table. "Yeah, well, I didn't think that would work, anyway. I can never get the stupid water snake to go faster than a crawl."

"Why did you try to kill me?"

"I knew as soon as I saw Mark back here. When I realized you were at the Makepeace Circus, I was sure someone would spill the beans. Deo is an idiot," she complained. "Come to think of it, Leo is an idiot, too. I'm surprised the two of them pulled the kidnapping off at all, to be honest."

Fortuna returned with Mark and Serena. The lioness's golden eyes stared daggers at Alexa, and her mouth hung open with a vaguely predatory expression. Even in humanoid form, an unmistakable aura of danger flowed from her.

"I should tear the flesh from your bones," Serena whispered. Mark wrapped an arm around his girlfriend and tried to calm her.

"Yeah, you could try. You'd just wind up lapping up water," Alexa retorted.

"How many seconds does that transition take you, naiad?"

"Okay, I realize everybody's angry and annoyed—"

"Annoyed, ringmaster? I burn with the rage of a wronged mate! The betrayal of this water sprite can *never* be forgiven." Mark stepped in front of Serena and placed his hands on either side of her head, bending her into his chest. Caressing her neck, he whispered and soothed her to calm down.

"Rage and vengeance will not help solve the problem."

"You don't even know what the problem is." Alexa crossed her legs on the couch and bounced. "My little adjunct plan may have failed, but the Witches Council will take you right the heck down, ladies."

"Why do you hate our life so?" Anya exploded. She advanced on her sister, a combination of rage, fear, and sadness dripping through her words. "This place gave us family when our parents were killed by those same witches you now suck up to! We were given a home! How could you betray us? What happened to you, sister, that you are gleeful while ripping Alessandra and me from our home? While killing? While siding with the very same people that destroyed our family?"

"You have the nerve to ask me that?" Alexa rose and stood toe to toe with her sister. "We are owed so much more than a yurt and a boat ride for what we went through! Traipsing across the country, but always being outsiders! Living in a place where we could never have the power we are due as naiads! A place we could never lead? A home we can never conquer? Tethered to this place like slaves?"

"You could leave anytime that you wanted to, and you did!"

"It's not enough. I hate this place. I hate we are the enemies of the most powerful beings in the paranormal world because we live here. And for what?"

"For loyalty! We are enemies of our parents' murderers! And for Poseidon's sake, what freedom do you have now?"

"I don't need freedom," Alexa laughed. "I've got a condo."

"And I'm a lawgiver and have a seat on the Witches Council," I interjected. "Doesn't approval to live in Impy require a unanimous Council vote?"

"It does at that," Anya agreed, her face breaking into a smirk.

"You do not! They would never let you vote!" Alexa looked alarmed. "They already voted! You can do nothing!"

"Maybe not. But maybe they have to let me vote. Maybe as a lawgiver, I can imprison you. I'm not even sure what powers I have yet, but I'm almost sure I can do something. You know it, too, don't you?" I asked her. "That's why you tried to kill me."

Alexa stared daggers at me.

"That's the funny thing about cleaving to laws and traditions," I shrugged. "Sometimes, those laws and traditions can cut both ways. We'll find out soon enough."

I was grateful for all those political science classes I took in college. It seemed like those would come in handy. Maybe even more usable than a magic book.

"It won't matter," Alexa said, recovering her

composure. "You won't figure out the solution to keeping those two humans alive in time, anyway. And once they are dead, everyone here will know you cannot protect anyone. If you cannot protect them, the Magical Midway will collapse from within, even if you don't lower the barrier. And then you are no lawgiver. The Witches Council won't even need to lift a finger to take you down."

The conniving naiad stared at me. She stood straight and tall. Triumphant. Arrogant. With a haughty assurance, as if there was no way she could lose despite being caught dead to rights.

"There *is* a solution, then?"

Alexa's face fell, and her shoulders slumped ever so slightly.

"I told you once your ego would be your downfall, sister," Anya told the younger woman wistfully.

"And so it may have come to pass," Serena said.

After binding Alexa and handing her over to the Larry brothers, the group reconvened to discuss the solution. Despite Anya's pleading with her sister, Alexa refused to reveal to us what she knew. The restriction against my using magic to gain knowledge seemed concrete and immutable. No amount of magic words or hand-waving could make her talk, and I was unwilling to engage in any form of torture to compel her (though Serena was insistent it was called for).

Off to the Magical Midway jail, she went. After we made some watertight adjustments.

We were joined by Fiona and Ningul, and Uncle Phil and Samson. Avalon didn't meet us. Anya let us know she was busy trying to calm the deer herd down.

"I don't know why I would be relevant to the Witches Council at all," Mark told us as we crowded around him. "Why me and not Fortuna? I have no idea. I'm just a mind-reading human, not all that valuable at all. I can't even read the minds of other paranormals, so I am certainly no threat to them."

"And yet you are a threat to them," I pointed out.

"My sister never specifically said Mark was a threat. Just that he was somehow key to whatever solution there is to get the Witches Council off our backs."

"Well, they like to be on our backs, so that's a threat to them," Fiona said. Ningul nodded. "They didn't give her a condo in Impy because of her delightful personality. She pledged to do something for them."

"Something serious enough to risk getting blamed for this," Uncle Phil agreed. "The Witches Council isn't supposed to kidnap paranormals."

"You keep telling me what the Council is supposed to do and not supposed to do. What happens if the Council does something it's not supposed to do? Does fire rain from the sky? Does a Titan rise out of the earth and scold them?"

"People would lose all regard for the Council," Fiona replied.

"Would the Council care?"

Everyone gawked at me.

I was often astonished at how my rational and straightforward questions caused such consternation and bewilderment in my friends. I cared about everyone here, but for goodness sake, these guys had blind spots you could drive a Mack truck through.

They have lived this way for hundreds of years, Charlotte, Samson said. *You are coming from an altogether different approach than they have had. They've had no opportunity in their lives to question how their world works. You are awakening questions they have never had. It's unsettling for them. Have compassion, Ringmaster.*

I have tons of compassion!

You are incredulous. Try being understanding.

You know, you are not the most exceptional example of empathy and understanding, Samson.

Do as I say, not as I do. There's a reason that a cat is not the ringmaster. Though believe me, I pleaded for it. Vociferously.

"Look, all I'm trying to say is I think you guys are making presumptions about what the Council would or wouldn't do that may not be true." I sought to sound patient and less judgmental. "Take nothing off the table, and assume nothing."

Better.

Bite me.

Samson's claws unsheathed slightly into my leg in response.

"I get it," Mark said and nodded. Of course, Mark got it, he was a human. "I honestly can't think of any reason I would be important, Charlotte. I mean, I've only known about the paranormal world for a year, really. Before, I was just a nerdy college professor." I raised my eyebrow.

"A professor of what?"

"Paleography and Manuscript Studies. I have a

Ph.D. in it, actually. Like I said, I was just a big nerd."

"So, ancient documents?" Mark nodded.

"I studied medieval documents connected to folklore regarding changeling children. I guess even before I knew what I was, something in me leaned toward those old stories." Mark shrugged. "I always knew I was different, I suppose. Even when I didn't really *know*."

"Refresh my memory. What's changeling folklore?"

"Many cultures believed elves or fairies would exchange their own children with human children. There are stories in Ireland, Germany, Cornwall, the Isle of Man. Some people theorize it was used to explain children born with disabilities. Now, I wonder if some of the stories were due to halflings like myself."

"Halflings, changelings—are these terms the ones generally used? Like, are they the proper terms?"

"I think so," Fiona said. Serena nodded.

"That's how I have always heard those terms used. And though there are other words, those are the most common, I think," Anya agreed.

"There are stories, less known and less common, that marks changelings as human children that have been turned into elves or fairies."

"That's it!" I shouted.

"What's it?"

"I know how to beat the Witches Council. And holy glitter mounds, are they going to be *ticked off.*"

CHAPTER 12

DESPITE REQUESTS FROM THE ASSEMBLED GROUP, I didn't tell them what my idea was that night. It had been a long day, and I wanted to talk to Roland Makepeace before divulging my plan. Alexa was safely locked away where she could do no further damage, but the clock was ticking down on our confrontation. I needed sleep.

My dreams were fitful. I rarely had vivid, intense dreams. Often my sleeping hours were filled with images of home. I relived moments with my parents playing in green fields with happy dogs, dinner out with my friend Tabatha. Movies with my friend Aiden. They were muted images in my head, comforting memories I could snuggle into while I slept.

This dreaming? This was something else.

I was draped in a soft white robe. Gentle white light glowed from everywhere and nowhere. It danced on the dense fog that curled around me.

"Are you going to take your first step, Charlotte? Will you join them?" The words sounded as if they were coming from twenty voices layered on top of one another. Harmonious and musical, they didn't frighten me.

"I don't understand." My voice sounded hollow compared to the rich, layered texture of the voice coming at me through the fog. "I'm walking. I don't know where I'm going. I can't see anything."

"You can see more than is before your eyes. You can hear more than sound. You know more than you think. You are connected to more than you know."

"You're confusing me. Is this a dream? Or is this real? Who are you?"

"Are you going to take your first step, Charlotte? Will you reach out?"

As the question echoed in my mind, the voice faded away along with the light.

I awakened the next morning feeling troubled by the odd dreams. When I laid my head down on my pillow the night before, I was confident I had solved the riddle. I would beat the Witches Council at their own game and had hit upon a solution that would solve everything. I was sure of it.

Then the dream came. Now, I felt like I was missing something.

"Back to the Makepeace Circus this morning, my girl?" Uncle Phil stomped into my yurt without asking. "It's almost 9:30 in the morning, sleepyhead. The Witches Council will return tomorrow evening. While I have no doubt you have solved the entire affair, I will feel a lot better once you explain how you've done it."

"Oh, ye of little faith," I said, crawling out of bed. Uncle Phil handed me a coffee cup, and I sipped. "Just plain coffee? Really?"

"Sometimes the traditional serves the purpose. How long do you think you'll be gone?"

"Two hours at most, I think." I stepped into my changing booth. Anya had enchanted a shower box for me a month ago. As soon as my clothes were removed, it blasted me with water from every direction. Admittedly, it felt a little like being a car in a car wash, but in a mere six seconds I was cleaned, coiffed, and perfumed. There was something to be said for quick convenience.

"Do you want me to go with you?" my uncle called as I slipped on my clothes.

"No, I'm fine," I told him. "I don't think I'll have any problem whatsoever. Gunther's expecting me, and I imagine he's talked to his father by now."

"I wouldn't assume that," Uncle Phil mumbled.

"What was that?"

"Nothing, dear girl, nothing at all," he hollered.

"We need to get my parents here." I emerged from the cleaning box and sat down in a chair to put my shoes on. "Frankly, I may have screwed up by not getting them here to start. The closer we get to the deadline and the more we learn, the less I trust Mina's word about respecting the seven days."

"I'll talk to Jeannie and get them here," Uncle Phil nodded.

"Call them on the cauldron first."

"Why, Charlotte, what fun would that be? I haven't made my younger brother upset with me in a while. It will be just like old times." I sighed and shook my head. "It's all in fun young lady, all in fun. In times like these, we should find our fun where we can. We are circus people. It's in our nature!"

"I don't know that my Dad has the same view of what's fun, Uncle Phil," I told him and I stood up. "Okay, I'm going to get out of here. Is there anything you need from me as the duly authorized supply closet for the Magical Midway, before I go? Hay? The redecorating of a yurt? Chocolate from Paris? I can do it all."

"No, you just—actually, chocolate from Paris sounds wonderful. Maybe just a bar before you go? It would make a wonderful gift for Jeannie."

"She's a genie. She can magic up a chocolate bar from Paris any time she wants."

"But if I bring it to her, it's completely different," Uncle Phil pointed out.

He had a point.

I held out my palm and concentrated, asking for the most delicious, expensive bar of Parisian chocolate to appear in my hand. Before I could even blink, it appeared, and my uncle snatched it up with a bow.

"Thank you, dear girl."

My last thought before I transported myself

to the Makepeace Circus was that I would probably get very fat now that I had discovered how easy it was to magic chocolate into existence.

Parisian chocolate.

Yum.

Ambom glared at me when I turned up at the gate of the Makepeace Circus.

"Wish I could attack you," he grunted. "You big disappointment as intruder, witch."

"Sorry about that, dude." I grinned. "I'm glad that you won't attack me, though. I would much rather be your friend."

"Friend? You want be Ambom friend?" The dark monster with the glowing red eyes walked up to me. The slobber dripped from his maw as he tipped his head like a dog.

"Sure, why not!" I turned my head away from the monster's horrible breath that bathed me in waves of stink. "We're all circus folks, right? Why not be friends?"

"I never had witch friend before," Ambom mused.

"Well, now you do. I need to talk to Roland

and Gunther, though. Do you know where they are?"

"In circus somewhere." Ambom waved behind him. "You my friend now. You go."

"Thanks, Ambom." I smiled and nodded.

As soon as I stepped onto the grounds, I saw Ethel Elkins shuffling toward me with an intricately jewel-encrusted cane. The old woman ambled, hunched over, but a chill ran through me when her eyes connected with mine.

"You've returned!" I returned her smile, but the cold continued to run through my body. Although I had seen Ms. Elkins at the meeting a few days ago, she could not have seen me. I hadn't brought my body, and I was supposed to be invisible. "I told you it begins." She nodded and cackled to herself.

"I'm sorry, ma'am, I think you have me confused with someone else. I don't believe we've met." The old woman smirked as I walked toward her. "I'm Charlotte Astley, the ringmaster of the Magical Midway."

"Oh, I think you know that I know you just fine. How did you sleep last night, young lady?" The old lady cackled as my face froze. "Any interesting dreams?"

The large old lady was hunched over, gnarled

hand clenched around her cane. Two dark eyes peeked out at me over old-fashioned wire spectacles. Her face was a map of lines topped with a wild shock of white hair.

As I came close to her, I also realized she was at least ten feet tall. How did I not notice that the other night? Wait, she was shorter than Gunther then. What the heck?

"I, uh..."

"What's the matter, girl, cat got your tongue?" the gigantic old lady said. She took two rickety steps forward and shoved her wizened face into mine. "Never seen a norn before? Huh? Have ya?"

"No, ma'am," I snapped in response, standing straighter. Holy crow, this old lady was intimidating.

"I've seen your fate, girly." She backed up and shook her cane in my direction. "Destiny is a funny thing when it comes like a thief in the night. Two big balls," Ethel Elkins cackled. "Brighter than stars, and planted in the earth. Boom! They won't know what hit 'em."

I stared at the old woman in confusion.

"Who are you?"

"Oh, I'm just old Ethel, young one. No one special. No one special at all. No one listens to the jabbering from an old woman. You can safely ignore me."

It was all I could do not to burst out laughing. At this point, I felt there was almost nothing in the paranormal world I could safely ignore. As I considered what I would say to her next, Gunther popped out from behind a cotton candy stand.

"Hey, thought I heard murmurs of an interloper ringmaster wandering around." He smiled as he came up to Ethel and me.

"I think I literally took twenty steps into your circus so far."

"Yeah, well, everyone's getting even more on edge than usual. Just a little. Good morning, Ms. Elkins. How are you doing this morning?"

"Oh, you're such a handsome boy, Gunther Makepeace. And sweet, to greet a little old lady with such friendliness. Are you taking our girl to see your father?"

Our girl?

"Yes, ma'am. I don't want to be rude, but we need to get going. I know that Charlotte is in quite a bit of a hurry."

Ethel shuffled and turned her steely eyes on Gunther. "Don't think old Ethel is crazy anymore, do you? Didn't I tell you? Of course I did. I told you. I'm not greedy, I tell, I tell. You thought old Ethel was just a crazy old lady. Norns know. We know more than you think." Ethel pinched Gunther's cheek and chuckled. "Are you ready for it? You should be ready!"

"Ms. Ethel, that's not what we're here about," Gunther said as his eyes shifted in my direction.

"You don't want to talk about the future, hmm? No talking of fate, no talking of destiny? No karma, no kismet? You youngsters, always looking back. What is to come is where you *should* look! Not behind you. Not even to this morning of the past," the white-haired woman said, shaking her finger at us.

I stared at the old woman, trying to follow what she was saying, but it was as challenging as getting Fiona to calm down. Gunther clearly did, though.

"Ms. Ethel, you know I love you, but we have to go. Time is running out, and we have a lot to discuss with my father."

"We all are running out of time, now, aren't we, Gunther? Time just ticks away. Tick tock tick tock." The old woman smirked as if she knew far more than she was saying and whirled away from us while whistling. "You two hurry on now," she called over her shoulder. "Time's a-wastin'."

"That is a very, very strange old woman," I

told Gunther while we watched Ethel Elkins sashay away.

"You don't know the half of it," Gunther admitted.

"It won't work," Roland Makepeace barked at me, pacing in his living room.

"I think it will. If they can do it, or threaten to do it to my parents, then we must be able to do it, too. It ensures that they can't come after us, or you."

Gunther sat on the couch, his face white. His emotions were so chaotic I couldn't get a definite read on how he felt about my proposal. His father's confidence in our failure was not helping to calm him.

"Look, neither one of us have delved into the full range of the ringmaster power. I can do things that you don't do. It's not because you can't do them but because no one has thought to do it in your line. I suspect that you can do things that I don't do, but I could if I tried. If a human being with a tiny drop of paranormal blood can walk onto our grounds and be smacked with a full-blown paranormal power, we have the power of transformation. We do it all the time."

"How so?"

"Did you hire an architect to build all this? When you move, do you run it with a convoy?"

"Don't be daft, young woman. And don't treat me like I'm stupid. I've been a ringmaster longer than you've been alive." Gunther's father scowled at me. "These are all things."

"These are all things that were manifested or transformed. I'm telling you, it will work. The ringmaster power transforms us so that we can't be hurt as easily. So that we have powers far beyond what any regular witch can do. It's all the same principle. It's just transforming one thing into another thing."

"I'm not risking my son's life on your harebrained scheme to outwit the Council!"

"Okay, then let's test my hypothesis. We have two people that committed crimes, one each. Get Deo. I'll get Alexa and Leo. Let's try it out."

"You're very glib about changing a paranormal's very essence, Charlotte," Gunther breathed without looking up. "Even as a punishment, I can't agree with what you're proposing to do as a test. I can't allow someone else to risk their life."

"Gunther Makepeace, don't you dare! What this girl is saying—"

"Makes sense, Dad." Gunther rose up to face him. "It makes sense, and you know it. If you and Charlotte can pull this off, not only does it protect Mark and Fortuna's lives, it safeguards both circuses. And it makes sure that when you're gone, there is a successor to the Makepeace Circus. An heir that can, without question, receive the ringmaster power."

"Gunther," Roland choked out as he strode toward his son. "I can't risk your life. I can't lose you. I lost your mother. What would she say if I lost you as well? You are all I have left of her..." Roland Makepeace enclosed his son in his arms.

I felt awkward. This was a desperate, warm side of Roland Makepeace I had never seen before, and I could feel his anguish. The man had carried his wounds buried deep within the rage and smugness that wrapped around him like armor.

"Dad, we have to try this. Charlotte's right. But I can't let anyone risk their life for me. You need to do this. Now. Before I get cold feet and change my mind."

"I can't—"

"You have to."

Silence settled in the room, and I was afraid to breathe. Roland hesitated and squeezed his son once more, ruffling his sandy colored hair as if he was a boy. Stepping back, Roland held his hands up and concentrated in his son's direction.

Nothing.

"Must be doing something wrong," Roland muttered.

"Try again, Dad."

Roland took a deep breath and raised his hands again, palms out toward Gunther. This time, energy sparkled along his skin as he stared into Gunther's eyes. His face was tense with the effort as he concentrated.

Nothing.

"I told you it wouldn't work," Roland snapped at me.

"It has to," I told them. "We're doing something wrong. If they can do it, we have to be able to do it."

"I'll take care of my own here, young lady." Roland Makepeace walked over and grabbed my arm to steer me toward the door. "Each circus has a ringmaster, and each ringmaster has a job. That's how it's always been, that's how it will always be. You go worry about your own problems and leave us alone."

My brain echoed with Roland's isolationist statement, but other words from my subconscious bubbled up and bounced against his pronouncement.

Of course.

"You're wrong." I shook my arm from his grip. "I know you're wrong. Yes, that's how it's always been. But it hasn't worked, don't you see? Once we were so many circuses, and now there are just two. Just us. Do you understand? It can't be that way anymore."

"Get out." Roland opened his front door. "Get out, and leave us alone. Go tend to your own crisis. Let us tend to ours."

I tried to call to Gunther, but the heavy wooden door slammed in my face.

"You gonna let those men treat you like that?" Ethel Elkins called from across the path.

I was right. I knew I was right.

I just had to prove it.

CHAPTER 13

"IT'S NEVER BEEN DONE BEFORE," UNCLE PHIL TOLD ME AGAIN.

"But there's no reason it can't be done. No addendum, no preclusion, no rule, no law. No explicit reason it can't be done. There is no specific thing that will happen if I try and do it. Right?"

No, Samson said.

"That's good enough for me. We need to go back there now. How do I do this?"

"Just think what you want. No humans are left at the fairground since the witches showed up with their threats, so everyone is here. You just need to ask for what you want and focus. The Magical Midway should do as you request."

I closed my eyes. *I want to move the Magical Midway to a safe position next to the Makepeace Circus. Our new location should adjoin the Makepeace Circus. I want this done now.*

I felt the energy shift and settle more quickly than any move I had ever made before. The midway itself seemed…concerned and restless. Eager, even. I stepped out of the yurt quickly and got past the carousel to look toward the western boundary. "It's not there."

"Look, Charlotte, to the east. It's behind the Sticky Walls ride." Uncle Phil pointed toward the werepens and a centrifuge ride that used science, not magic, to stick riders to walls. The ride was now outlined against another carnival. A larger, taller, fancier carnival. I swallowed my jealousy.

"Come on, let's go see if we can make a doorway," I dashed across the clearing near the children's petting zoo. As Uncle Phil, Samson, and I sprinted toward the Makepeace Circus, Fiona and Anya ran toward us.

"What on earth is going on? Why did we move? And why on earth are we next to them?" Anya asked as soon as she was within hollering distance. "Are we trying to make sure that the Witches Council has one big target to hit when they thrust a lightning bolt at us?"

"If they throw lightning bolts at us, we'll both be fine," I told her as Fiona and Anya jogged with us. "I have figured out how to solve the Witches Council issue, but I need to convince Roland Makepeace, and the circuses have to be near each other."

"Good luck convincing that daft jerk of anything," Fiona jogged toward the barrier.

"There." I pointed toward a place that the spheres adjoined. There was ample room on either side to craft a passageway. "If no one sees a better spot, I'm going to put a tunnel here."

"Can you do that without their agreement?" Fiona asked.

I looked at Uncle Phil. He shrugged. Samson said nothing.

"I guess we'll find out," I responded.

No one spoke, and I closed my eyes to ask for a tunnel that would allow the paranormals in the circuses to pass back and forth between the two properties' protection. I opened my eyes, and an extended half circle led straight into the Makepeace Circus. A gargoyle head appeared around the side at the other end.

"Ambom?"

"Yes, lady ringmaster," the gravelly voice screeched through the tube.

"Get the other gargoyles and go to the ringmaster's cabin. Tell Roland and Gunther what I did, and bring them here. Can you do that?"

"He gonna be mad?"

"Probably, but eventually he won't be," I hollered.

"I go do that right away. You be here?"

"I'll be here."

"Charlotte," Fiona asked, "why are we connected to the Makepeace Circus? What in the world is going on?"

"I promise I'll explain, but I need you to go get Mark and Fortuna. Bring them back here as quickly as you can." Fiona looked as if she wanted to argue with me, but she nodded and went racing toward our yurts.

I hope you're right about this, Samson said.

I hope I'm right about this, too. If I'm not, I have nothing. No other ideas, no other solutions.

The tube was about ten feet tall and fifteen feet wide. I could see heads from the other circus peeking in, but no one traversed the path I had carved between the two carnivals. In the distance, an angry Roland Makepeace hurried toward the opening with Gunther in tow.

"Stay here, don't come in, and keep anybody

else from coming in," I told my Uncle Phil. I walked toward the halfway point, the dividing line that represented the infinitesimal barrier between our two circuses.

"What on earth have you done, young lady!" Roland roared as he entered the tunnel. His admonition echoed loudly, and I flinched.

"I told you, this will work. But we have to do it simultaneously."

"You must be out of your mind!"

"Maybe. But I still think it will work."

Roland and I came up to the line between our fairgrounds. It wasn't marked by anything, no energy or paint. No real indication it even existed, and yet both of us instinctively knew where it was.

"Gunther, I want you to stand right there," I pointed against one side of the circular-shaped tube. "Put one foot on that side, and one foot over here. Basically, I want one half of your body to be in each circus. You understand?"

Gunther nodded and his father continued looking at me with skepticism.

"Okay, Roland, stand over there and I'm going to stand over here next to you." I settled on the Magical Midway side and held out my hand for Roland's. He looked back and forth between

Gunther and me. With a sigh, he did as I asked and snatched my hand.

"We will try again on three. Ready?"

"I am, but I don't see how this could conceivably work…"

"One, two, three!"

Roland and I raised our hands concentrating on turning Gunther from a half-human witch to a full witch. Lightning bolts shot from our joined hands toward Gunther, and he stiffened, then rose two feet in the air. I felt Roland's hand relax as if he was about to pull away, and I clutched it tighter. "Concentrate! Don't let go!"

I felt Roland's hand stiffen in mine, and the colors that glittered through the lightning became deeper and sharper. The wind swirled around the three of us and my ears drummed with energy. It built, and strengthened, and crowded the small space. Suddenly my ears popped as the light flashed and then faded.

Gunther fell to the ground.

"Gunther!" I cried, dropping Roland's hand and racing to my friend. "Are you okay? Can you hear me? Gunther!"

"I'm…I'm okay. That was…something else." Gunther smiled. I helped him up off the ground, and he raised his eyes slowly toward his father.

"Did it work? I can't tell. Can you tell? Dad, did it work?"

Roland Makepeace stood stock still, staring at his son as if he had never seen him before. Tears rolled down his face and his hands shook.

"I could have saved your mother," Roland whispered. He covered his tear-stained face with his hands. "How could we have known? Why didn't we know we can do this? I could've spared her, Gunther. I could've made her a witch and saved her…"

"Dad, you didn't know."

"I should have known. All those years, all of the ringmasters so jealous of each other. So suspicious. Yes, son. It worked. I can sense the ringmaster tie, the blood bond, in you."

The two men embraced each other as one comforted, and one mourned anew. I fell back, leaving behind the two to process what had just taken place.

A bittersweet victory that guaranteed the endurance of Gunther and the Makepeace Circus. A win that came too late to save the mother they both loved.

～

"I don't understand," Mark said after I described to the group what had just happened. "You can make me into a witch? Is that what you're suggesting?"

"Well, not precisely. I mean, I can. Well, Roland and I can. But we can alter you into anything. If you preferred to be a cat, we could probably make you a cat. A giant. A wereshifter of any variety."

"We will no longer be human anymore?" Fortuna asked. I shook my head no. "And this will put us in conformity with the law?"

"Yes. You would officially be paranormals, just like anybody else."

"I think I need to sit down," Fortuna said, looking around. I summoned up a chair behind her at the edge of the tunnel. "This is a lot to take in."

"I get it, and normally I would give you more time to make a decision of this magnitude, but we have a day. Roland is here, and while I think relations between the Makepeace Circus and us are going to be better now, I don't want to bank your lives on it. Roland's here, we need to do this now."

"You have scant confidence in my gratitude, girl." Roland came out of the tunnel with

Gunther. "You have saved my son, and you have preserved my circus. It is clear that the old ways do not serve us anymore. Well, some of them."

"They never did, you old goat," Uncle Phil snapped at him.

"Aren't you dead? Do I still have to listen to your nonsense?"

"Thirty years ago I tried to make an alliance with you!"

"Thirty years ago you were an idiot."

"Oh?" Uncle Phil laughed. "Now I'm not?"

"Oh, you're still an idiot," Roland told my uncle. "Now you're not the ringmaster. She is."

Fortuna and Mark sat whispering with Serena. The two men quarreled and exchanged gentle insults about each one's intellectual proficiency. Gunther walked over to the three and leaned down, speaking with each extensively. Finally, all four stood up.

"I would like to be a lion shifter," Mark declared. "I know I will never find as loyal or loving a mate as Serena. The pride here deserves a better leader than someone that would betray one of its members, not to mention the circus." I nodded and Serena beamed.

"I...I don't know if this is allowed, but I would like to be a witch," Fortuna said shyly.

"I'm used to the way I look, and I don't know that I want to change that much. I just wish to be me, if I can. But not have people want to kill me."

Roland and I looked at each other and nodded.

"If you all will follow me into the transformational tube, we can get right on that," I announced.

"The transformational tube?" Gunther asked, laughing as he slipped into stride beside me.

"What? What's wrong with that?"

"Nothing. Nothing at all, Charlotte." He stepped in front of me. I stopped walking and stared at him.

Slowly, he stepped in to embrace me. Gunther's arms wrapped around me, and his hand caressed the back of my head through my hair. It was…an intimate embrace and shivers zinged up my spine.

"In fact, there's nothing wrong with anything today," he whispered. "Everything is just perfect."

"So, we're in compliance," I said, passing a plate of food down the large table. "But there's still the matter of Deo, Leo, and Alexa, and what we will say to Mina, Mabel, and Mercy."

"Why say anything to them?" Roland asked and grabbed some roast. The Makepeaces stayed for dinner so we could discuss our plans for the inquiry from the Witches Council, and my parents had joined us after being brought here by Jeannie.

Though we had solved all the direct violations of the law, no one here felt Mina, Mercy, and Mabel would be happy about that. "We should just keep our shields up, and let them rant away if they wish. They have no power over us."

"If we continue to isolate ourselves from paranormal governance, Mr. Makepeace, things will always stay the way they are," I pointed out. "We will always be playing this game of them coming after us and us defending ourselves."

"We've done fine with that so far," Uncle Phil said.

"I agree with the old goat," Roland Makepeace concurred.

"Maybe Charlotte and I don't want to spend our entire lives fighting a war," Gunther told his father and reached over to gently squeeze my hand. "They have destroyed or taken down every other circus in existence. If we keep doing things the same way? At some point, it will happen to us."

"This is why we left the paranormal world," my father told Gunther. "I felt that it was better for Charlotte to grow up in a place that didn't have the potential to break out into a war all the time."

"Alan, eat some of those vegetables," my mother pointed at his plate.

"Yes, dear."

"The human world has its conflicts," Roland said.

"Well, sure it does, but in most countries and systems there is a method to address grievances," I told him. "There are laws, judicial systems, elected officials, petitions. Rights to protest, even. I see none of that here."

"That's because we have none of that here," Uncle Phil said.

"Maybe Gunther and I don't want to be warlords in a dictatorship." Gunther nodded as he chewed.

"Then change it, Charlotte," Uncle Phil said, waving his fork at me with a mouthful of roast. "You have a seat on the Council now. Use it."

"I cannot believe you did that to your own niece," Roland Makepeace said. "Throwing that girl into that nest of vipers alone. You should be ashamed."

"I should? If you have such an issue with it, help her out. Make Gunther a lawgiver. It would be two against three, so Mina, Mercy, and Mabel would still have one vote on you, but it would give them a fighting chance." Uncle Phil turned toward Gunther and me, waving his fork at us. "Since you two are so much smarter than your elders and all."

"That's preposterous. I need the boy at the circus. We only tried to make him a lawgiver before to protect him. He's protected. Problem solved."

"Dad, I'm not a boy, you know," Gunther said, leaning away from me toward his father. "There's nothing you need me for at the circus, and you know it."

"Not true," Roland told him.

"Unless you're dead, that *is* true," Gunther countered.

"All right, then how about this? We just got out of one conflict with the Witches Council by the skin of our teeth. I don't want my son to go provoke another. This ring will not be worn by *anyone*."

Roland Makepeace reached into his front vest

pocket and pulled out a gold ring that looked very much like the one my uncle had given to me. He placed it on the table in front of him and pointed out it. "No one will be the lawgiver for the Makepeace Circus so long as I am the ringmaster."

Gunther reached over and grabbed the ring, turning it over and examining it. Without saying a word, he slipped it on his finger. Uncle Phil laughed so hard that tears rolled down his chubby cheeks. My parents looked at Roland Makepeace, who seemed to be in shock.

"What just happened?"

"I just joined the Witches Council," Gunther told me.

"Wait, what? How?"

"This isn't one of the more complicated magics of our world. You put on the ring, you become the lawgiver. It's as simple as that."

"Take that ring off your finger, Gunther Makepeace!" Roland shouted at his son.

Gunther held his hand out flat to his father. Roland grasped the ring and yanked, but could not budge it from his finger.

"Years and years ago when these were crafted, lawgivers got killed in the line of duty an awful lot. If someone tried to apprehend the criminal and got killed, their partner could simply slip the ring off the body and put it on their own finger to get the powers," Gunther explained. "Once the ring's on a finger, it's a done deal."

I reached down to tug my own ring off my finger. My skin pulled with it as if the jewelry had somehow fused with my body.

"Don't tug, Charlotte, it will just make your finger swell," Mom said.

"No, it won't, Martha," my uncle told her. "Your daughter is still invincible. The ring doesn't change that."

"You are a terrible influence on my son, young lady!" Roland told me, waving a fork in my direction.

"I disagree with you there, Dad," Gunther smiled and he turned to me. "Since Charlotte showed up, life has gotten pretty exciting."

Oh, barf, thought Samson.

CHAPTER 14

WE WAITED AT THE BACK OF THE CLEARING.

Roland and I kept our fairgrounds linked for the time being. Partly because we wanted to present a unified face to the wicked triplets, and partially because each circus was having quite a bit of fun exploring the other. I was also surprised to discover so many people had family members and friends at the Makepeace Circus.

Roland Makepeace was still dour, but the fury I had invariably felt rolling off of him under the surface seemed to have evaporated. While his sorrow at the loss of his wife, Gunther's mother, was still present, his rage and dread over Gunther's potential fate were gone.

Fortuna and Mark stood in the moonlight

next to Gunther. Roland, Uncle Phil and I stood in front of them. Everyone in both circuses knew of the confrontation due to take place. Though we were confident we could handle whatever came, we told anyone unnecessary to hide.

Just in case.

"The moon is almost in its proper place," Uncle Phil glanced up at the sky. "They should be here any minute now."

"In time to destroy you," Alexa mumbled from her containment box.

"Shut up, Alexa," Deo told her from the box next to hers. His brother Leo remained silent and paced within the cage.

"Did the naiad ever admit that the Witches Council put her up to the kidnapping?" Roland asked me.

"No." I shook my head. "Apparently, she *can* be loyal. She really didn't tell us much. Most of the information we got was from Deo. I don't think Leo knew much at all. He agreed because he hated Mark and wanted Serena for himself."

"So we know those three did it, but there is no proof at all they did it for the Witches Council."

"Pretty much," I nodded.

The darkness and silence were punctuated only by our low whispers. It seemed as quiet as the night I became ringmaster when the circus was transported between time and space.

"How are you three doing?" Uncle Phil asked Gunther, Fortuna, and Mark. The three nodded, but their tense limbs and concerned faces betrayed their anxiety.

"We covered everything, right?" I asked Roland and Uncle Phil. "I mean, we're not breaking the law, we got the people who kidnapped Mark. We're prepared for this in every way we needed to be. Right?"

"Charlotte, have faith," Roland said. Uncle Phil nodded. I bit my lip and stared out into the darkness.

They are coming, Samson said.

"Get ready," I told the others as light glowed just outside the border.

The first thing Mina did when she appeared was stare at Alexa caught within the magical containment box. The second thing she did was examine the sphered protection border, eyes narrowing when she realized it was still up. Once she glanced to her right and saw Fortuna, Mark, and Gunther lined up like lambs to the slaughter, concern disappeared from her face.

"I am pleased you decided on the wisest course," Mina called. Mercy and Mabel flanked her. Mabel looked as haughty and arrogant as ever, but Mercy stared at Gunther while biting her nails. "Take your border down so we can get on with this."

"Roland and I would like to announce a few things before we get started," I told Mina.

"Well, hurry up, then."

"The Makepeace Circus and the Magical Midway are currently in compliance with the Witches Council statute that states humans may not live at a moderated paranormal property."

"What are you talking about?" Mina asked, her eyes narrowed. "I see the three of them right there."

"Fortuna Delphi, as of yesterday, is a full-blooded witch. She is no longer human in any capacity, and therefore her residence here is not a violation. Likewise, Mark Botsworth is werelion and fully entitled to live here if we accept him. Which we have."

"What poppycock is this?" Mina stomped up to the border, stopping just short of the crossing. "They look the same as they ever have. What are you trying to pull here? Roland? Your half-breed—"

"Is also a full-blooded witch, and the unassailable, unquestionable heir to the Makepeace Circus," Roland told her. Mercy's eyes widened as Mina's narrowed even further.

"If this is some trick, Roland," Mina warned.

"No trick, Mina. If he was not a full-blooded witch, he could not wear the ring of the Makepeace lawgiver. If you direct your eyes to his finger, you will see he has been so elevated."

"No!"

"Yep," Uncle Phil said. "Mina, Mabel, and Mercy, please meet Charlotte and Gunther, the two newest members of the Witches Council."

I held up my hand and showed the ring. Mina's face twisted with rage.

"You cannot! You cannot sit on the Council!"

"Oh, they can, and they do!" Roland told her as he watched her twist and flail in frustration.

"I will never allow it!"

"Um, Mina, it's not up to you, remember?" Mercy told the angrier, larger woman. Mina whirled on the younger woman, but the shy girl stood her ground. "It's the law. They have the rings, and it's the law."

"Shut up, Mercy," Mabel snapped.

"We are the law!" Mina screamed.

"So are we," I shot back at the angry woman and stepped toward her. Gunther raced up to intercept me before I crossed the barrier, holding my arms to keep me from moving any further.

"Mina, get me out of here!" Alexa screamed and banged against the sparkling box. "You promised me!"

"Stupid naiad," Mina told her. "Shut up!"

Alexa whacked the box and paced like Leo.

"It doesn't have to be like this," I told Mina. She and I stared at one another across the barrier. "I don't want to have to constantly fight you. But I will if you keep running roughshod over your citizens and threatening them every time they turn around. Not to mention using them in plots against other people."

"Little girl, you have no idea what you walked into."

"Maybe I don't. But I know I'm not a little girl, and I know I'm not afraid of you."

I looked at Gunther and looked down at where he was holding me. He let go without my even having to ask him. I walked across the barrier and stood with Mina, Mercy, and Mabel.

"You started this plotting to take me down. To take us down. To destroy people's homes, to kill people to make a point. I don't agree with your leadership. I don't agree with how you run this place. I've been here three months, and I've seen nothing positive about the Witches Council. Nothing."

"You know nothing about us," Mina shot back.

"I know what's right. I know what's wrong. I know that people shouldn't be treated this way by those in power. I know if you're a leader and people run from you in fear instead of running toward you to build with you, you're not a good leader."

"You don't know what good leadership is," Mina said.

"Neither do you," I countered. "We are not in violation of the laws. You have no inquiry to make here. You failed in ruining us, you failed in dismantling what we stand for."

"There is always the next time," Mina said.

"See, you're proving my point. There shouldn't be a next time."

Mina stared at me, her breathing deep and loud. No one spoke.

"We're leaving," Mina told Mabel and Mercy.

"I'll see you at the next Council session on the quarter," I told her cheerfully when she turned away from me. "I'll bring donuts!"

Mabel and Mina disappeared. Mercy stood quietly looking at Roland from beyond the barrier. He walked forward and left the protection of the Magical Midway to embrace the quiet girl briefly.

"I'm sorry," she said as they pulled away. She inclined her head and looked up into his eyes with her own tear-filled ones. "Gerda would be so proud of you. I know she would. I wish I could say she would have the same pride in me."

Mercy wiped her eyes, glanced at me, took a deep breath, and disappeared.

"That didn't feel easy, but it was kind of easy," I told the group after the Witches Council left. "Honestly, I expected lightning bolts and some kind of magical explosion. This whole thing seems almost anticlimactic."

"Bite your tongue, Charlotte," Uncle Phil told me.

"What was that thing between you and Mercy?" I asked Roland Makepeace, who had returned to the protection of the Magical Midway and was embracing his son. "She's like a different person with you."

"I suppose she is at that," Roland sighed, turning from Gunther to face me. "Mercy grew up at the Makepeace Circus."

"I thought the only witches at circuses were the ones in the bloodline?"

"Just like in the human world, sometimes young people run away from their parents to seek fame and fortune or adventure. She arrived just before my father died, and he allowed her to stay. She's not as young as she looks."

"Dad and I have been talking a lot lately. Mercy was my mother's best friend when she was alive," Gunther added. "I didn't recognize her because she used a glamour when she was with us to hide from her family. I knew her as Raven. Anyway, she was devastated when Mom died and she left the Makepeace Circus shortly after. I'm still not clear on how she wound up with a seat on the Witches Council." Gunther looked at his father.

"Mercy is a Lawdottir. It's an old blood royal family in the witch community. I don't imagine it was too difficult once she went back to her family to take advantage of their political ties. And she did so, Gunther, to protect her best friend's son."

Gunther stared at his father.

"I thought her last name was World? And the three were sisters or something?" I asked.

"No, that's some affectation those women started," Roland said.

"You know, Charlotte, if Mercy has allies, we have a real possibility of changing the course of the laws in the paranormal world," Gunther pointed out.

"How do you figure? You and I are two people, and they are just three. There is another, what, ten members?"

"Those ten members don't even know what Mina is doing," Gunther pointed out and the rest of the group nodded. "It's common knowledge that Mina is running roughshod over the entire Council with Mabel and Mercy to back her up. The others just enjoy the palace and rubber stamp anything she does without even examining issues."

"You are the only two lawgivers. There used to be more. When there were many lawgivers the Witches Council was more like a parliamentary body. A hundred, maybe two hundred lawgivers sat as the voting body on the Witches Council. They could enact nothing without lawgivers," Uncle Phil explained.

"Now, they've consolidated power, but it's not

a *they* as in the whole Witches Council," Gunther said. "It's Mina, with Mabel as her right hand. If we can convince Mercy to come over to our side, it's just possible we could convince the others to get off their duffs and take back their power from Mina."

"I hate politics," Mark murmured.

"That's because you're a cat now," Fortuna told him. "I imagine there's a whole lot of things you are gonna lose patience for that you used to tolerate fine."

"Speaking of cats, maybe we should talk about the politics of our own circus right now before worrying about the rest of the world," Uncle Phil told the group, pointing toward the three containment boxes. "What are we going to do with them?"

Leo, Deo, and Alexa sat slumped in their boxes. Their attitudes and postures had changed.

Once the Witches Council left and you had bested them, I suspect the three of them realized they had no more allies, Samson sent.

"I feel like I want to start practicing what we're preaching."

"What you mean?" Gunther asked me.

"I don't want to be a dictator. Do you?" Gunther shook his head no.

"I quite like being a dictator, young lady," Roland Makepeace said as he crossed his arms. "Makes things easier."

"For you," I told them. "Not for anyone else."

"Well, of course for me! I'm the ringmaster!"

"Dad, you're always stressed and always angry. People are always afraid of you. What about that time you banished Blake and turned him into a frog? He didn't deserve that. You found out later he wasn't guilty of anything."

"Everyone makes mistakes," Roland murmured.

"If you had help, if we enlisted the people that are already leaders at our circuses, maybe mistakes like that wouldn't happen."

"We already kind of have something like that here at the Magical Midway," I told them. "When this started we gathered all the leaders together to talk about it. If we formalize that we have the beginnings of a more democratic way of doing things."

"This is human hogwash," Roland told me, waving me away like an annoying bug.

"We are a society the same way any other group is a society. We need to treat our people as members of that society instead of subjects."

"Dad, you can't expect us to go make a run on

the Witches Council and claim they should give us more freedom to self-determine when we don't even know how that would work."

"Well, I know how that would work," I mumbled. "I lived in a society where it worked."

"Like I said, human hogwash," Roland scoffed again.

"The humans have expanded across every corner of this planet, and we have done nothing but shrink in number for hundreds of years. We've lost towns. We've lost populations. We've lost circuses. We've lost paranormal species that will never be seen again. Maybe this is why. Maybe the humans know more than us. In this case, anyway," Gunther said.

Roland look surprised at his son's statement, as if he had never looked at the road paranormal history had traveled enough to follow it to its potential catastrophic conclusion. Deep in thought, the big man breathed heavily and nodded. "You sound like your mother, Gunther."

"I'll take that as a compliment." Gunther smiled. "Let's magic everything back to where it needs to be, and meet in Charlotte's yurt. We have a trial to put on tomorrow."

∼

"I didn't know you were so into politics," I told Gunther. We walked along the outskirts of the fairgrounds toward our gazebo. It had taken us two hours to hammer out a process for a trial that included a random jury, witnesses, and the whole nine yards. This process was informed by the many episodes of *Law & Order* I had watched over the years.

Oh, and yes, I said our gazebo, and yes, I realized I shouldn't. Heartburn. It must be heartburn. Please, please let it be heartburn.

"I don't know that I am," he told me. "What I do know is I spent so long hating the way my father ran things, wondering if it could be done differently, and fearing because I was half-human I would never get the chance to try. In one day, Charlotte, you changed all that for me. You gave me hope."

"It wasn't me. It was your father and me, together. I don't think just one of us working alone could have changed anything enough to avoid what would happen. No matter how powerful we think we are."

"That's the point, though, isn't it? You see things here so differently. You see possibilities and improvements. The rest of us have been so conditioned to just accept the way things are and to handle them within the confines of what we see as immutable."

"Yeah, I have to admit I don't understand that," I told him as we climbed up into the gazebo and sat down. "You have all grown up with magic and power. So many possibilities, so much ability to transform your own reality. And yet you're locked into these traditions as if they can never be changed."

"Maybe not so much anymore," Gunther smiled. I smiled back as my heart pitter-pattered in my chest. Gunther reached out and brushed a stray hair from my cheek. "You're incredible. I've never met anyone like you."

"I, um, yeah, thanks," I said, turning my head away. "You're a great friend, Gunther, and I don't know I could have gotten to this point without you."

"A great friend," Gunther murmured, sighing. "Yes, I will always be your friend, Charlotte. I consider it a great privilege. I didn't have many friends growing up, or even at the circus. Our relationship has been significant to me, too."

Oh. My. Gosh. That's it.

As a half-witch, Gunther had probably not had many opportunities to date anyone. If the past few days have taught me anything, it's that the prejudices in this community ran deep. They were followed long past anyone remembering the reason for them.

Of *course*, he had feelings for me. I was probably the first female he had gotten close to.

It was just that, and nothing more.

Now that Gunther was a full witch, his world had opened up to him. I knew as soon as we traveled to Imperatorial City, the handsome ringmaster heir would beat off single witches with a stick. I swallowed that knowledge down and tucked it in with the heartburn ball that bounced around my gut every time he looked at me.

I think you're—

Samson, please don't. On this subject, just please don't.

But—

No.

But I think—

No.

CHAPTER 15

THE TRIAL WAS AN EXCITING, IF WEIRD, SUCCESS.

Alexa was banished to the prison at Democritus for masterminding the entire kidnapping. The members of the jury were not impressed with her excuse she was destroying us for her own betterment. Why she thought an explanation would impress them, I have no idea.

"What will happen to her?" Anya asked me as Lucius Larry led her away.

"Honestly, the paranormal prison isn't that bad," I told Anya. That morning, I added a door in the communications yurt that would lead to the intake area at Democritus. The prison looked like a stripped down beach resort. Their philosophy seemed more containment of villains and protection of citizens than punishment.

"Will I be able to visit her?"

"Yep, as much as you want. There's even a pool and some activities for you guys to do together to try and help you bond. I was surprised. Considering how lackadaisical Mina seems to be about causing people's death or kidnapping, I was expecting something much less humane."

"Maybe it will give Alexa some time to think about the choices she has made in her life."

"That's the hope."

As Leo and Deo were brought to the defense box for sentencing, Mark stood up and asked if he could speak to the jury before they passed sentence. Ari Riddle, who was serving as the judge, nodded. Mark turned and stared into the faces of those that populated our hastily built jury box.

"I realize that these two men have broken the bonds of trust with the circus. I also realize that there must be consequences to those actions and that you have been entrusted in this process to impose those consequences." The crowd in the gallery quieted to listen to the newly minted lion shifter.

"I ask you to have mercy on these young men. They are young and foolish, and in the end, I was not harmed. They could have hurt me, and I was nothing more than a human at the time. I believe they can be redeemed, taught right from wrong, and become responsible citizens of our world." Leo and Deo stared at each other in shock as Mark Botsworth spoke elegantly for mercy.

"If Leo cedes, voluntarily, the leadership of the Magical Midway lion pride to me, I will accept them as members of the pride and take responsibility for their moral and ethical correction," Mark said. Serena sat behind Mark and smiled proudly as her mate showed everyone what she had always seen in him.

"In a way, I am indebted to them. I am now who I was always meant to be, and with the person I was always meant to be with. That might never have happened if these two had not done what they had done. I would like to repay that. Thank you."

"Such mercy from a victim of such treachery, I think everyone here would completely agree," Ari Riddle said. "Leo and Deo, first, I must ask— would you abide those conditions if given that task?"

Leo nodded, his eyes wide. Deo jerked his head once without looking up.

"Jury, I charge you now in deciding their fate. Will you allow for Mark's mercy, or jail them with your mandate?" The sphinx stared at the jurors, who whispered to one another and nodded. Brownie Brown stood up.

"We believe these young lions deserve a chance to improve themselves if they can. Our sentence is to entrust them to Mark and Serena." Leo and Deo broke down weeping, clasped their hands and thanked the jury.

"As the Judge of the Magical Midway, I say court is adjourned. May you all take lessons from those truths we have learned." Ari Riddle slammed a gavel I had ringmaster-magicked up, and the crowd clapped as if a play had just concluded.

"Well, apparently, I have lost a lion to you, girl," Roland Makepeace said as he walked over with Uncle Phil. "I already see the short end of the stick on this deal!"

"I think who we each wind up with may all shake out. Look." I point to the edge of the clearing where centaurs, goblins, and kelpies from both circuses were gathered, talking. "I suspect some more people may switch circuses."

"Still…" Roland grumbled.

"That was quite an interesting spectacle, Charlotte," Uncle Phil said. "A judge, a court, a jury. How did Ari Riddle wind up the judge?"

"A quick show of hands election this morning while you slept. I think eventually, we'll want to formalize it, but most of the citizens here chose Ari. Then they drew straws to sit on the jury."

"It was a good choice," Gunther said. "He seemed to do well."

"Ari's a good man," Uncle Phil agreed.

"Did you outsource your job as lawgiver?" Roland asked.

"I don't see it that way," I disagreed as we walked toward the communication yurt. "I see it as helping folks get something in place where they don't need a lawgiver."

"Or a ringmaster?" Gunther asked.

"Don't be silly, boy," Uncle Phil said. "We couldn't undo this magic if we tried."

"Have we ever tried?"

"Well…no…"

"Look, I'm not some anarchist crazy human-world witch who wants to tear everything down. I just think a lot of the problems I see in the paranormal world are because everything is locked in some ancient set of rules that no one even knows the reason for anymore." I walked into the communications yurt where Alexa slumped on the couch in handcuffs, waiting for transport.

"Well, I'm glad you don't want to tear everything down," Roland said. "Realize that your motives may not be so clear to others."

"Nothing good ever came easy," I told him, putting my arm around Anya. She stared at her sister, a single tear escaping her eye.

Alexa stared back at her, beaten but defiant.

"I should have known," Anya said later that night when we gathered around the table. Fiona, Fortuna, Avalon, and Anya had arrived for a girls' dinner. Serena, a new addition to our group, sat quietly and periodically glanced at the door.

"We all have a blind spot where family is concerned," Fiona told our sad friend. The normally boisterous, tough Anya looked pale and deflated. "I should not have snapped at you about her. None of us wish to believe those we love could do such things."

"I don't want to talk about it any more," Anya snapped, and Avalon squeezed her hand.

"Then let's talk about boys. Holy hair, did you see Mark when he shifted into a lion?"

"No, and I hope I do not," Avalon said and shuddered.

"Mark would not eat you, deer-woman," Serena told her without looking up from the table. "My mate is an honorable man and a true leader. It was fate he come to this place to become what he is. What I think he always was."

Avalon leaned away from Serena, still adjusting to the new predator at our table. Well, the only predator, really. "Does he not hunt?"

"Of course he hunts! We are lions," Serena said, raising her eyes. "Our yurt has a door to the plains of Africa. We do not hunt paranormals. Though I would have gladly lunched on Leo given a chance."

"You didn't agree with Mark's plea for mercy?" Fortuna asked her.

"No, witch, I did not," Serena answered, and Fortuna blushed with embarrassment and pride at the new designation. "My mate is wiser than I am, however. And he is the leader of the pride."

"I still don't get that whole male-only leader thing," Anya said, showing a little bit of her old spunk. "What makes him so much wiser than you?"

"Well, in this case, he grew our pride by two members, ensuring we are stronger. While I would have ripped the throats of Leo and Deo both, making our pride smaller and that much closer to extinction."

"Fair point," Anya said. "You know, I kinda like you."

"You are more tolerable than many," Serena responded with a nod.

"Do you really think you and Gunther will change the way things are, Charlotte?" Fortuna asked, passing the carafe of human wine down toward me. It amazed me that with so many incredible magic drinks, my girl group loved everyday old human wine.

"I don't know," I sighed. "I talked to my parents before we sent them back home, and my Dad thinks I'm crazy. All these things, the drama, the plots, the rules. That's some of why he left and went to the human world. He thought it was more civilized."

"We're not barbarians!" Anya said. Fiona looked at Anya and raised her eyebrow. "Well, maybe a *few* barbaric tendencies."

"No one should be afraid to step out of a protective circle because some ruling group might hit you with a lightning bolt because they don't like you." The women around the table looked at each other and nodded. Fiona reached out and touched my arm.

"When's the next Council meeting?"

"At the quarter, so a few months from now, I think?"

"They will have apoplexy when Gunther walks in."

I looked at Fiona. "Why?"

"He's a *man*," Anya said. "They don't allow men on the Council."

"They can't not, can they? I mean, he's a lawgiver."

"You two may have the only two lawgiver rings left in existence after the Council of old made it a point to destroy as many as they could. I don't know if they can stop him now that it's on his finger. But a man hasn't sat on that Council for nearly a hundred years, and it will raise their hackles."

"Looking forward to it," I said, and raised my wine glass. "To raising hackles and shaking things up."

The six of us clinked our glasses and spent the rest of the night talking about boys while Samson slept peacefully on my bed.

"That's better," Gunther said. I hovered the hairbrush in midair. "Now move it slowly—remember, no fire hose. Trickle out just what power you need and remain calm and relaxed, not tense."

I breathed deeply and tried to keep my muscles relaxed. The hairbrush skittered a quarter inch at a time in fits and stops, but it didn't fly across the yurt, and nothing got broken.

"Good! Except you're jerking your fingers, and your energy. You want to smooth the edges and even out the flow. Here." Gunther stepped behind me and wrapped his arms around my body so he could grip my wrists. I could feel his muscled chest pressing into my back and—

The brush shot across the room and shattered the mirror.

"Sorry! Sorry, I got distracted," I told him, blushing. Gunther waved his hand at the mirror, and the pieces jumped back into place. As Gunther turned toward me with a smirk, Fortuna popped her head in.

"Everything okay in here? I thought I heard something break."

"Everything's fine, Charlotte's just struggling

with distractions," Gunther told her. I continued to hide my red face.

"Oh, okay," Fortuna said. She continued to stand in the doorway. "Hey, um…would you guys mind if I watch the lessons? I'm super new to this witch thing. I know that it was done just to save my life, but since I have these powers, I'd really like to learn to use them."

"I don't know why I didn't think of that!" I ran to the door and dragged her in. "Gunther, you don't mind showing both of us, do you? Fortuna knows even less than I do about all this stuff."

And maybe adding a third to this mix will put distance between the handsome Gunther and me, so I will stop having this heartburn and hyperventilation issue.

Gunther's face remained steady, but I could feel he wasn't happy with my suggestion. Competing feelings of obligation and desire wrestled within him. Necessity won, and he smiled at Fortuna. "Of course. The more, the merrier, and you're right. It's something you should learn."

"I don't want to intrude," Fortuna said, backing up, and staring at Gunther. Apparently, Fortuna had gained intuition ability with paranormals now that she was a witch.

"Stay," I grabbed her arm, refusing to let go. "It will make it much easier for me if I'm not the only one breaking mirrors. And we can practice together in between lessons."

"Okay, if you're sure," Fortuna said, raising an eyebrow. I nodded and hugged her. "Ow, you're squeezing me really hard, Charlotte."

"Sorry! Sorry."

As Gunther held out the hairbrush and explained to Fortuna how to control it, Samson broke into my thoughts.

That will not help, you know.

What?

Just because you added Fortuna to this educational mix doesn't mean the feelings you two have for each other will just disappear.

We don't have feelings for each other.

I live in your head, Charlotte. Lie if it makes you feel better, but I feel it my obligation to inform you that it's a futile gesture.

Fortuna smiled at me as Gunther grabbed her arm to help her with the movements, and I grimaced.

Things are changing, Charlotte. Perhaps a relationship between you both is not as hopeless as you think.

Nothing's changed.

Something has changed.
Oh, yeah, cat? What?
You.

Go grab **Unbearable Magic**, the next book in the Magical Midway series right now!

KEEP UP WITH LEANNE LEEDS

Thanks so much for reading! I hope you liked it! Want to keep up with me? Text me at 1-512-359-3123 to get updates, info, or to shoot me a question!

You can also visit leanneleeds.com to:

Find all my books...

Sign up for my newsletter...

Like me on Facebook...

Follow me on Twitter...

Follow me on Instagram...

Thanks again for reading!

Leanne Leeds

FIND A TYPO? LET US KNOW!

Typos happen. It's sad, but true.

Though we go over the manuscript multiple times, have editors, have beta readers, and advance readers it's inevitable that determined typos and mistakes sometimes find their way into a published book.

Did you find one? If you did, think about reporting it on leanneleeds.com so we can get it corrected.

www.ingramcontent.com/pod-product-compliance
Lightning Source LLC
Chambersburg PA
CBHW031612240626
47153CB00002B/726